"Okay," K... "You can ... ...

Brock slowly slid out from under the bed, his dark hair slightly tousled. "It's been quite a while since I've hidden under a girl's bed." He smiled. "Makes me feel seventeen again."

His smile made her stomach feel funny. "Glad to know I'm not your first." Kate held out her hand to help him to his feet, her heart skittering at the way his big hand closed around her fingers.

"Thanks," he said, straightening to his full height.

"You're welcome," she replied, automatically reaching up to brush the dust bunnies out of his hair. Suddenly she realized just how intimate her actions were and drew back her hand as if she'd been burned. "Sorry."

"Me, too," Brock said huskily. "I'm sorry you stopped."

Kate swallowed, the tone in his voice making her skin tingle. *It's the skirt,* she reminded herself. Brock wasn't really attracted to her. He was just reacting to the skirt's magnetic qualities.

But after seeing how good he looked in her bedroom, Kate was tempted to take Brock any way she could get him....

Dear Reader,

Do clothes make the man, or in this case, the woman? Most people think so. As a poor college student, on the first five dates I had with my future husband, I actually wore clothes I borrowed from friends. I really wanted to impress him, and I was sure that nothing I had in my meager closet could do the job. And I wouldn't be surprised if young women today were having the same problem. Wouldn't it be great if there was a special store that sold clothes guaranteed to attract men?

In *Seduced in Seattle*, Kate Talavera doesn't find the store—but she gets The Skirt! And she's determined to use it to catch the man of her dreams. Only, when she meets sexy Brock Gannon, her dreams begin to change....

I hope you enjoy the third installment of the SINGLE IN THE CITY miniseries. Cara Summers, Heather MacAllister and I had so much fun writing them! And the fun isn't over yet! To find out more about our ongoing series, check out our Web site at: www.singleinthecity.org.

Enjoy,

Kristin Gabriel

Books by Kristin Gabriel

HARLEQUIN TEMPTATION
834—DANGEROUSLY IRRESISTIBLE

HARLEQUIN DUETS
7—ANNIE, GET YOUR GROOM
25—THE BACHELOR TRAP
27—BACHELOR BY DESIGN
29—BEAUTY AND THE BACHELOR
61a—OPERATION BABE—MAGNET
61b—OPERATION BEAUTY

SEDUCED IN SEATTLE
Kristin Gabriel

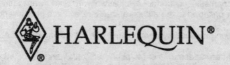

HARLEQUIN®

TORONTO • NEW YORK • LONDON
AMSTERDAM • PARIS • SYDNEY • HAMBURG
STOCKHOLM • ATHENS • TOKYO • MILAN • MADRID
PRAGUE • WARSAW • BUDAPEST • AUCKLAND

This book is for Brenda Chin—
editor, adventurer and friend.

ISBN 0-373-25968-9

SEDUCED IN SEATTLE

_____Prologue_____

FATE WAS CONSPIRING against Kate Talavera. There could be no other reason she found herself locked in the ladies' room of the reception hall the very moment the bride was scheduled to toss the skirt.

"Let me out of here!" Kate pounded on the bathroom door, hoping someone could hear her over the loud music reverberating from the reception hall. The strong odor of pine-scented air freshener was giving her a headache.

When her fist grew sore, Kate leaned against the sink and debated her options. Staying stuck in the ladies' room wasn't an option. Not when an event that could change her entire future was about to take place.

She glanced at her watch, noting that it was almost time for the bride, Gwen Kempner, to toss the bouquet. But Kate didn't care about that. She wanted the skirt. The secret weapon that had snared husbands for all three of her old college roommates.

The skirt came from an island hidden deep in the Caribbean and a rare, powerful thread ran through it. A thread that drew men to the woman who wore it and entranced them forever.

Wearing the skirt, which she had caught at Torrie's wedding, Chelsea Brockway had found true love with Zach McDaniels and been married at Christmas. Kate and Gwen had both been bridesmaids, only Gwen was the one lucky enough to catch the skirt that night. Shortly afterward, Gwen had met Alec and this morning, on Valentine's Day, she had become Mrs. Alec Fleming. Now it was Kate's turn.

If she could get out of the bathroom.

She looked around the small lavatory for some kind of tool that she might be able to use to pry the door open. But all she found were some extra rolls of toilet paper and an empty tube of lipstick. This couldn't be happening. Not when she'd finally found the perfect man.

Todd Winslow, her former next-door neighbor and the current owner of one of the most successful home shopping channels on cable television. He was smart, successful and, best of all, single. In two weeks, he'd be coming to Seattle to attend her parents' fortieth wedding anniversary party.

That's when she planned to snag him. All she had to do was catch the skirt, then catch Todd. She'd waited so long for true love that she wasn't about to let a locked door stop her now.

Kicking off one shoe, she whacked the three-inch

heel against the edge of the sink until the small rubber tip on the end of the heel came loose. She pulled it off, then rubbed one finger over the sharp metal point. She'd chisel her way out of here, if necessary.

A knock sounded on the door, sending a rush of relief flowing through her. Kate dropped her shoe and ran to the door, pounding as hard as she could on the solid wood. "Please, help me! I'm stuck in here."

"Kate?" Chelsea's familiar voice drifted through the door. "Is that you?"

"Yes, it's me. Have I missed it yet?"

"No, but Gwen's been stalling until I found you. She can't hold off much longer. Alec is more than ready to start their honeymoon."

"You've got to get me out of here!"

"Okay," Chelsea replied through the door. "Hold on and try to stay calm. I'll get Zach and see what he can do."

Kate paced back and forth across the porcelain tile floor. She had to catch the skirt. At twenty-seven, she'd kissed more than her share of toads in search of a prince. And endured yet another Valentine's day without a date. It was time to take her future into her own hands.

"Zach tracked down the manager," Chelsea called through the door. "He's getting a key."

"Tell him to hurry."

"I can't believe this is happening to you," Chelsea said, laughter bubbling in her voice.

"I can." Kate slumped against the door. "This kind of thing happens to me all the time. I find a decent guy, then fate steps in and snatches him away."

"I think you're exaggerating just a little."

"Then how come the last guy I dated got transferred to Hong Kong? And the one before that got hit by a car?"

"That's terrible," Chelsea exclaimed. "Was he killed?"

"No. The car was only going five miles per hour. But he fell in love with the emergency room nurse who treated him. They were married six weeks later."

The door was finally opened by a grinning Zach. Chelsea pulled Kate toward the reception hall. "Let's go. Hurry!"

Kate kicked off her remaining shoe, then rushed out into the decorated hall, noting the excited group of women gathered in the center of the room. She could see Gwen standing on the balcony above them, her new husband next to her.

Elbowing her way through the crowd, Kate did her best to ignore the growls of displeasure and dirty looks all around her. Gwen gave her a relieved smile when she finally saw her, then tossed the skirt high in the air.

Kate watched it float toward her, almost in slow motion. She boxed out her competition, just like her big brother had taught her to do when going up for a rebound in basketball. Adrenaline and hope fueled her leap as she reached up to snatch the skirt out of the air. She pulled it down. The unusual fabric felt soft and silky in her hands.

Victory.

Until the woman standing next to her, a buxom blonde wearing a gown with huge shoulder pads, tried to grab it. "That skirt should have been mine."

"Sorry, it's mine," Kate said firmly, tightening her grip on the skirt. "I caught it."

"Possession is nine-tenths of the law," the woman said through clenched teeth, giving it a hard tug.

"Be careful!" Kate exclaimed. "You're going to..."

The sound of tearing fabric made the words die on her lips.

Chelsea arrived, her eyes wide with horror. "What happened?"

The blonde dropped her end of the skirt, then pointed accusingly at Kate. "*She* tore it. Now it's probably ruined." Then she stomped away.

Kate held up the skirt to survey the damage. "It looks like it's just ripped a little at the side seam. All it needs is some mending."

Chelsea nibbled her lower lip. "I'm not so sure, Kate. It's the thread that makes it special. I don't know what will happen if you mend it with plain old cotton thread."

"Don't worry." Kate squared her shoulders. She had the skirt and that's all that mattered. "I'll think of something."

1

BROCK GANNON walked into Dooley's Bar and looked through the smoky haze. He didn't feel any of the old excitement at embarking on a new mission. Maybe turning thirty had something to do with it. Or the fact that nothing seemed to challenge him anymore. He specialized in recovering stolen goods that the police couldn't, or wouldn't, find. Of course, sometimes the clients didn't want to involve the police, especially if a relative was involved in the theft.

Working as a mercenary had taught Brock to suspect everyone and trust no one. It was a cynical attitude, but it had kept him alive and well for the past eight years. His occupation was a dangerous one, since it often brought him into the company of thieves and other lowlifes. But it had made him a very wealthy man and had taken him all over the world, including exotic places where few civilized people ever ventured. But somehow, he always found his way back here to Boston, to Dooley's, although he didn't really have anywhere that he could call home.

Brock's boss worked out of this bar, owned it in fact, having retired from the mercenary field himself. Now Sam Dooley simply supervised the missions, assigning the best man or woman in his employ to the job, and taking a small percentage of the fee for himself.

A haunting Irish melody emanated from the jukebox and two men sat at the long oak bar, each of them staring into his mug of dark beer. The sound of a woman's laughter drew Brock's attention toward the back of the bar. A billiard game was in progress and he spotted the snow-white hair of his boss as he bent over the table to rack up the balls.

Brock ordered a beer, then ambled over to an empty booth to wait until the billiards game ended. He wasn't in any hurry. He'd spent enough nights in empty hotel rooms to appreciate the change of scenery.

Thirty minutes later, Dooley approached the table. "Well, hell, Gannon. Why didn't you let me know you were here?"

Brock nodded to the two women at the billiards table. "Looked to me like you were busy."

"You could have joined us." Dooley sat down across from him, raking his shaggy white hair off his forehead. "Made it a party."

Brock shook his head. "I have to catch a plane

early tomorrow morning. Although you didn't mention where you're sending me this time."

"Seattle."

Brock picked up his beer and took a long swallow. He knew Dooley was watching him, waiting for a reaction. Too bad he'd be disappointed. Seattle was now just another pit stop in a long line of cities. London, Chicago, Toronto. They all blended together after awhile.

He'd grown up around Navy bases in different parts of the country, including Whidbey Island. His mother was a Navy groupie, taking dead-end jobs in towns near a base in hopes of enticing an enlisted man into marriage. She'd caught five, but thrown them back when they'd failed to make her happily ever after. His own father hadn't even bothered to stick around long enough to see Brock born. Dooley was just one of the four stepfathers who had tried to fill the void. His favorite one.

"Speaking of Seattle, I talked to your mother on the telephone yesterday." Dooley motioned to the waitress for another round of beers. "She told me she received an invitation to the Talaveras fortieth anniversary party. You're invited, too."

Brock nodded, though he had no intention of going. He'd cut all ties with Seattle the day he'd left twelve years ago. Dooley knew all about the Talaveras. Knew how close Brock had been to them before he enlisted in the Navy in the middle of his senior year. Tony Talavera had been his best friend the three years Brock had lived in Seattle. Tony's family had opened up their home to him.

He stared at his empty beer mug, remembering Sid and Rose and Katie the Pest, Tony's little sister. She used to have her nose buried in those gothic romances, escaping to her room whenever Tony would tease her about them. It all seemed like such a long time ago.

Their waitress approached, breaking his reverie. Brock sat back and waited until she had set the frosty beer mugs down in front of them and walked away again. "So tell me about this mission."

One corner of Dooley's mouth twitched. "It's a little unusual."

"Then it sounds like my kind of job." Brock's special skills as a military tracker had made him one of Dooley's best operatives.

At first, Brock had thrived on the recovery work. The travel to exotic locations. The one-night stands with beautiful, mysterious women. But somewhere along the way, his job had lost its allure. It all just seemed so pointless.

He'd thought about quitting, since he didn't really need the money anymore. But then what? Brock knew he was at a turning point in his life. Unfortunately, he had no idea which direction to go.

He leaned back against the booth. "Who's the client?"

Dooley took a swig of his beer, then wiped the foam off his upper lip. "A native of Calabra."

Brock knew about the tiny island nestled in the Caribbean. The people liked to keep to themselves, never exploiting their beautiful beaches or tropical forests for the hordes of tourists that flocked to the other, more well-known islands. Few people even knew of Calabra's existence.

"This woman is one of the candidates in a special election there," Dooley continued. "Apparently, she believes recovering the item will win her votes. She promised to pay top dollar and kept emphasizing the importance of keeping this transaction confidential."

Brock arched a brow. "Don't we always?"

Dooley nodded, then picked up his mug and grinned. "But guess what she wants?"

"What?"

"A skirt."

Brock waited for the punchline, but Dooley just kept grinning at him. "A skirt?"

"That's right. And get this...I received another inquiry about obtaining the same skirt. Only this customer was too skittish to give his name and quickly backed off when I quoted him our usual fee."

Brock held up one hand. "Wait just a minute. What the hell are you talking about? What skirt?"

"A woman's black skirt. Made out of some weird kind of black fabric with a zipper in the back and a slit up the left side. I've tracked the skirt from New York City to Houston and now my sources tell me it's reached Seattle. Your mission is to secure this skirt and turn it over to our client in Calabra as soon as possible."

Brock stared at him for a long moment, then laughed "Sully put you up to this, didn't he? He's still peeved because I found that old Egyptian papyrus after he'd been searching for it for eight months."

"This is legit, Brock."

"Come on, Dooley. Give me a break. A skirt? Now, if I was supposed to find a woman *in* a skirt, that might be a different story. I do have certain skills in that area."

"And you might need them for this job. I told you it was bizarre."

Brock stared at him over the rim of his mug. "You're serious."

"Damn serious. Apparently, there is a rare thread that the natives of Calabra believe has special powers. This thread is woven throughout the fabric of the skirt. It was never supposed to leave the island."

Brock still wasn't buying it. "Special powers? Are we talking about voodoo?"

Dooley shook his head. "More like a love charm or some such nonsense. According to this client, whenever a man sees a woman wearing this skirt, he's entranced forever. The client's afraid of the havoc the skirt could wreak on an unsuspecting public. Or at least, that's the story she's telling."

Brock grimaced. "A skirt that binds a man to a woman forever. Sounds like my worst nightmare."

Dooley chuckled. "It's all a bunch of superstition. I'm still amazed at what people will spend their money on. But apparently this client has tried other avenues to secure the skirt and failed. I promised her that you could get the job done."

"I'll admit I've been called a skirt chaser a time or two, but never quite this literally."

"It gets better. Or worse, depending on how you look at it."

"Don't tell me, let me guess. I have to find matching shoes for the skirt?"

"No, but you do know the woman who has it. Kate Talavera."

Brock stilled. "Now you have to be joking."

"Afraid not, Brock."

He leaned forward. "Are you telling me Kate *stole* the skirt?"

Dooley shook his head. "No, nothing like that. It's been passed through several people since it was smuggled into the country."

Brock breathed a silent sigh of relief. He didn't want to think of Kate, or any of the Talaveras, involved in something ugly. Their warmth and friendship was one of the few memories he had that was untarnished.

Brock pushed his beer away. "Why didn't you tell me the Talaveras were involved right from the start?"

"Because I was afraid you wouldn't hear me out."

"You were right." He stood up. "You'll have to find somebody else to do this job."

"Are you sure that's what you want?" Dooley asked as Brock headed toward the door.

He slowly turned around and moved back to the table, his jaw clenched. "I'm not going to steal from the Talaveras. I'm not going to lie to them, either. And you know I'd have to do both to do this job."

"I know it," Dooley said bluntly. "And I know they're important to you. Hell, that's why I came to you first. You know better than anybody that I don't tell my people how to do their job. If someone else goes out on this assignment, then it's completely out of my control. They'll use whatever methods are necessary to get the skirt. And you know what that means."

Dooley didn't have to spell it out. Brock knew all too well that Kate or any of the Talaveras could possibly be hurt in the process. Kate's home could be ransacked. Or worse.

"Hell, Dooley." Brock raked one hand through his hair. "I don't want to do this."

"That invitation to the anniversary party is the perfect opening. Make a vacation of it. Catch up with some old friends."

Brock shook his head. "No way. I'm going to find the skirt and get out of Seattle. If I'm lucky, none of the Talaveras will even know I was there."

"Does this mean you're taking the mission?"

"Do I have a choice?"

Dooley squinted up at him, his head cocked to one side. "You always have a choice. You can just walk away. Pretend I never even brought it up."

But Brock knew that would be impossible now. "Do I have any competition to worry about? Did the second caller go looking for a better deal?"

"It's possible," Dooley said slowly. "Did you know the Weasel is going solo now?"

Brock nodded. "I heard something about it." The Weasel was a mercenary who had worked for a top agency in London. But he was too volatile, so they'd let him go. Now he was working out of the U.S., making cut-rate deals to drum up business. The Weasel didn't care who he hurt to accomplish a mission. Brock didn't even want to think about what would happen if Kate Talavera got in the Weasel's way.

All his old memories about the Talaveras came flooding back. Part of him wanted to see them again, although he knew Tony was in Brazil now, working for an export company and recently married. How would Tony feel if he knew Kate was in possible danger? And that Brock had turned his back on her?

Brock picked up his mug off the table and drained it. "I'll take the mission."

"Good." Dooley held up his beer. "To success."

Brock had never failed at a mission yet. The key was proper planning and keeping a cool head. Tomorrow, he'd catch a plane to Seattle. Then he'd scope out the territory. The first item on his agenda was locating Kate's residence. Hopefully, she'd be in the telephone directory, making his job a little easier. If not, well he still had a few contacts in Seattle. He'd find her place one way or the other.

After that, his job would be simple. He'd wait until the house was empty, then search the place until he found the skirt. If he was lucky, and he'd depended on luck more than once in this job, he'd be on an airplane to Calabra by tomorrow night.

So why did Brock have a sinking sensation that his luck had just run out?

2

KATE STOOD in front of a long mirror in her old bedroom, staring at the new secret weapon in her fashion arsenal. The skirt she'd caught at Gwen's wedding fit perfectly. She turned to the side, thrilled that the mended seam was invisible, thanks to her mother. The thread she'd used was almost an identical match. Almost.

The question was, did the skirt still work?

Her stomach grumbled, reminding her that it was her lunch hour. A meeting planner for one of the biggest hotels in Seattle, she normally munched on leftovers from business brunches. But the hotel was full of prospective models today, interviewing for a local talent agency, so the catering menu had been limited to baby carrots, assorted dried fruits, and bottled spring water.

A diet she'd endured herself during her college years, trying to shed all those unwanted pounds she'd carried around as a teenager. A combination of low self-esteem and an Italian mother who loved to cook had led Kate to balloon up to almost two hundred pounds by the time she was fifteen years old.

Now she was a perfect size ten, the same size, ironically, as her petite mother, who never gained an ounce from the high calorie meals she made. Kate smiled to herself, remembering how Rose had entreated her to move home again after Kate's apartment building had been sold to a condominium developer. She'd gained five pounds just thinking about it. So instead, she'd chosen to stay in a suite the hotel made available to its employees.

But she didn't intend to stay there much longer—*if* the skirt still worked. She smoothed down the silky black fabric, the key to winning the man of her dreams. Todd Winslow had been the golden boy at her high school—football captain, senior class president, National Honor Society. He'd been her next-door neighbor since they were both in elementary school, and was always unfailingly polite to her. Not like so many other boys who heckled her about her weight.

But he'd never really noticed her either. And she'd forgotten about him after high school, when he'd moved to California. Until six months ago, when Todd, who owned a successful home shopping network, had invited three of his most influential teachers to appear on the show. Rose Talavera, a retired high school math instructor, had been one of the three.

Upon her return, Rose raved about both the trip and Todd Winslow. Gushing over the courteous way he'd treated her and hinting broadly to Kate that he was perfect husband material. Kate had seen Todd on the show and agreed. He was even more handsome now than he had been in high school. With her mother's glowing recommendation ringing in her ears, Kate had made an impulsive decision to invite him to the anniversary party. She'd been shocked when he'd accepted the invitation. Especially since he would have to travel over eleven hundred miles from Los Angeles to attend.

Todd had sent his RSVP via e-mail, and they'd been corresponding that way ever since. His messages were both funny and flirtatious. Kate had never thought that she could attract a man like Todd—but now she had the skirt. The *altered* skirt.

How could she find out if it still worked? The sound of a jackhammer pounding the pavement outside gave her the answer. She'd stroll the sidewalk and see if the construction workers noticed. Of course, a few of them had made catcalls and whistles when she walked into the house so it might be hard to tell. But it was still worth a shot.

Taking a deep breath, she turned and opened her

bedroom door, running straight into the man who stood on the other side of it. Lurching back, she screamed as he reached out and caught her by the shoulders.

"It's all right. I didn't mean to scare you. It's me. Brock Gannon."

Her heart beating wildly in her chest, she took a deep breath, trying to subdue the adrenaline rush. "Brock?"

It simply couldn't be him. Brock Gannon was a skinny teenager with a black leather jacket. This man wasn't skinny. And he wasn't a teenager. He stood well over six feet tall and his broad shoulders almost spanned the doorway of her room.

"Brock," she said again. "Is it really you?"

He nodded. Then his gaze dropped down her body, rising ever so slowly again until his gun metal-gray eyes met hers once more. He opened his mouth, but no words came out. He just stood there, staring at her with a look of stunned disbelief on his face.

"What are you doing here?" she asked, her mind whirling. Brock hadn't been in the house for over a decade. At one time, he and her brother Tony had been inseparable, sharing a love of fast cars and even faster women. He'd certainly never given Kate, a chubby teenager with pigtails, a second look.

But she'd been a little wary of him anyway. He'd

always dressed like a tough hood, with clothes that never seemed to fit his gawky body. He'd never talked much either. And she knew he'd gotten into his share of trouble. It all culminated when he got in a fight his senior year in high school—with Todd Winslow of all people—and had been expelled. Brock had joined the Navy the next day and she hadn't seen him since.

How ironic that the boy he'd beaten up was the man she'd been fantasizing about just a few minutes before. She wondered if Brock even remembered Todd Winslow, or knew how well he'd done for himself. But judging by his expression, Brock didn't even remember her.

Then a slow smile curved his mouth, transforming his face into one of the most handsome she'd ever seen. "Katie the Pest? Is it really you?"

She took a step closer to him, surprised to feel a slight wobble in her knees. She held out her hand. "It's just plain Kate now."

"Hardly," he breathed, grasping her hand and pulling her toward him for a hug.

Kate sucked in her breath at the hard strength of his body. Brock Gannon had definitely grown up. She felt the scrape of his whiskers against her cheek and the contour of his finely honed biceps beneath her fingertips. At last, she stepped away from him, a blush warming her cheeks. From the way he was staring at her, she wasn't the only one disconcerted by the unexpected reunion.

Then it hit her. Brock was looking at her like that because of the skirt. It obviously still worked. But rather than relief, she felt a twinge of disappointment. Brock probably wouldn't have given her a second glance except for this skirt. The adrenaline rush she'd felt at his arrival began to fade away and the question she had when she first saw him standing outside her bedroom door came back.

"How did you get into the house?"

He hesitated a moment. "The door was open."

She shook her head. "I can't believe I forgot to lock it." She must have been so excited about trying on the skirt that it had completely slipped her mind.

"I just walked right in." He smiled. "I guess old habits die hard."

She knew her parents' house had once been like a second home for Brock. His own home life had been less than ideal, according to her brother Tony. The tiny apartment he shared with his mother was in a seedy part of town, most of their furniture and clothes secondhand. His mother worked nights as a cocktail waitress, leaving Brock to fend for himself. Which was why he'd spent most of his time at the Talavera's house.

But that was over a dozen years ago. She found it a little odd that he had just walked right in and up the stairs to her bedroom. "What brings you to Seattle?"

He hesitated a moment. "I came for the party."

"Oh." She'd sent an invitation to his mother, asking her to pass it along to him, but hadn't heard a word from either of them. "I never got your RSVP, so I just assumed you weren't coming."

"I hope it's not a problem."

"No, of course not..." The sound of voices emanating from the living room made her grab his arm. "It's Mom and Dad! They can't see you here."

His brow furrowed. "Why not?"

She pulled him into her bedroom, then swung the door shut. "Because then they'll know something is up. I'm throwing them a surprise anniversary party. If you suddenly show up after all these years, I know they'll suspect something."

"Do you want me to climb out the window?"

"You'll break your neck if you do. I'm on the second floor. Just stay in here until the coast is clear." A knock at the door made Kate jump.

"Katie, can I come in?" Rose Talavera asked from the other side of the door.

"Just a minute, Mom." Kate whirled toward Brock. "Get under the bed!"

"How about the closet?"

"There's no room in there." She pushed him down toward the floor, then watched him scoot under the bed.

Her father's voice emanated from the hallway. "Why are you standing out here, Rose? Where's Katie?"

"She won't let me in," Rose replied.

"Are you all right in there, Katie?" Sid Talavera called through the door.

"I'm fine," she shouted as she straightened the bed ruffle to conceal the six feet, two inches of male hiding underneath. Then she sat down on the edge of the mattress. "Come in."

The door opened and her mother and father entered the room. Sid was a building contractor, his burly frame a testament to his profession. Rose was a head shorter than her husband, with full, pink cheeks and a ready smile.

Rose looked around the bedroom. "I thought I heard you talking to someone."

"Just myself." Kate stood up and twirled around. "Thank you for fixing the skirt, Mom. It's perfect."

Sid frowned. "It's a little short, isn't it?"

Rose smiled. "So, some men like to see a bit of leg. What's wrong with that?"

"All I'm saying is that there's not very much material there. And I don't know why both of you have been so excited about this skirt. I was expecting to see sequins or something a little more dazzling."

"It's subtle." Rose reached out to brush at a small spot near the hem. "Men like subtle. And they like legs. It's a good combination."

"I still say my Katie doesn't need some magic skirt to win a man. They should be falling at her feet like flies."

Kate's cheeks burned as she thought of the man currently laying in the proximity of her feet. She never should have told her parents about the skirt. Or it's effect on men. But she couldn't worry about that now. She had to find a way to get Brock out of the house without her parents seeing him.

"Well, some men need a shove before they will fall," Rose said, rising to her daughter's defense. "And if the skirt can help give them that shove, what's the harm?"

Sid still didn't look happy about it. "So what exactly are you planning to do, Katie? Stand around in shopping malls and cruise the aisles of Safeco field during a Mariners game looking for men?"

"A Mariners game?" Rose shook her head. "Baseball season doesn't even start for two months. I think she should strike while the skirt is hot. She's been a bridesmaid in two weddings since Christmas, thanks to this skirt. Now it's our Katie's turn to be the bride."

"Don't worry, Dad," Kate assured him. "I don't plan to go trolling for men. I've got one picked already."

Rose's eyes widened. "Who is it? Do I know him? What does he do for a living? Does he come from a nice family?"

Kate held up both hands. She'd already said more than enough. Certainly more than she wanted Brock Gannon to hear. "I know you'll like him, Mom, but that's all I'm going to say for now. He may not be interested in me."

"If that's the case," Sid replied, "then he's too stupid to be my son-in-law."

"I need to change now," Kate said, glancing at her watch.

Sid and Rose moved toward the door. Her mother turned on her way out. "Let me wash that spot out of the skirt. I was making cannoli while I was mending it and must have spilled a little dab on the hem."

"That's okay. I'll take it with me and wash it out later. I've got to get back to work."

Rose looked disappointed. "I was hoping you could eat lunch with us."

"Sorry, Mom. There's a big meeting of investment

bankers scheduled later this afternoon and I need to check in and make sure everything is ready."

Sid rubbed his hands together. "So that means more cannoli for me."

Rose tutted under her breath as she followed her husband out of the room. "You get one cannoli, Sid Talavera. I mean it. And don't try to sneak one past me like you did last time..." Her voice trailed off as they moved down the hallway.

Kate walked over to the door and closed it. "Okay. You can come out now."

Brock slowly slid out from under the bed, his dark hair slightly tussled. "It's been quite awhile since I've hidden under a girl's bed." He smiled. "Makes me feel seventeen again."

His smile made her stomach feel funny. "Glad to know I'm not your first." She held out her hand to help him to his feet, her heart skittering at the way his big hand closed around her fingers.

"Thanks," he said, straightening to his full height.

"You're welcome," she replied, automatically reaching up to brush the dust bunnies out of his hair.

He took a step closer to Kate as her fingers rippled through the short, silky strands of his hair. She suddenly realized how intimate it was and drew her hand back as if she'd been burned. "Sorry."

"Me, too." He said huskily. "I'm sorry you stopped."

She swallowed, then turned around. "I need to change clothes, then I'll find a way to sneak you out of the house. Do you have hotel reservations somewhere?"

"Every place I checked was full. I was hoping I might stay here."

She turned to face him again. "That won't work. Not if I want to keep this party a surprise. And you're right about the hotels. February is a busy convention month is Seattle. I work as a meeting planner at the Hartington."

"So I heard."

She nodded, aware that he'd heard every word of the conversation with her parents. She wondered why he hadn't asked about the skirt yet. After all, even she would admit it was a little bizarre to believe a skirt could find you the man of your dreams. She'd still be a doubter if she hadn't seen the effects for herself. On the other hand, maybe Brock was used to desperate women and wanted to steer clear of the subject.

"Most of my time at the hotel is spent coordinating business meetings and conferences, but I also organize parties and receptions. That's where my parents anniversary party will be held." She planted her hands on her hips. "Which is still two weeks away. What do you plan to do in the meantime?"

He shrugged. "See the sights. Take a trip out to Whidbey Island. Reacquaint myself with the city..." His gaze lingered on her. "And old friends."

It was the tone of his voice more than his words that made her skin tingle. It's the skirt, she sternly reminded herself. Brock didn't really want her, he was just reacting to the skirt's magnetic qualities.

"I might be able to squeeze you into a room at the Hartington," she said, quickly changing the subject. "We usually have one or two last-minute cancellations."

"Sounds perfect."

"Good. Then I'll just change clothes and we can be on our way."

"Need any help?"

Kate blushed, a little surprised at the obvious strength of the skirt's seductive powers. "I'm old enough to change clothes all by myself now, Brock." She gathered up the linen pantsuit on the bed and headed toward the door. "But thanks for offering."

She opened the door, then closed it again. "Can you believe it? My parents are still out there arguing about the cannoli."

He moved up behind her. "I can see Sid's point. Your mother's cannoli is incredible."

His warm breath caressed her neck, sending a delicious tingle throughout her body. She swallowed hard, then peeked again through the crack in the door. "They just disappeared into their bedroom. Their door is closed. Now is your chance to make your escape. I'll run interference if they come out before you make it to the front door."

"Okay," he said, moving into the hallway. But his gaze was still fixed on her.

"Go," she cried, giving him a shove. "Before they see you. I'll meet you this evening at the Hartington Hotel on Yesler Way."

He smiled. "I'll be waiting."

3

BROCK FOLLOWED Kate into the lobby of the Harting-ton Hotel, his eyes glued to the sexy sway of her hips. She wore a pantsuit now instead of that skirt, but he could still envision the long, slender line of her legs. The way the silky fabric of the skirt had molded to her sweetly curved rear end. He imagined himself fitting his hands there, her body moving against him...

He mentally shook himself. Brock had been attracted to women before, but he'd never let it affect his mission. And his mission was simple. He had to get his hands on the skirt. Unfortunately, it looked as if he'd have to get close to Kate to do it.

That wasn't part of his plan.

Whenever possible, he tried to avoid contact with people during a mission. It tended to make things too unpredictable. And potentially dangerous. His normal routine was to research the object he'd been hired to recover, map out a strategy for obtaining it, then leave the vicinity before anyone was the wiser.

Only nothing had gone right with this particular

mission from the start. His research hadn't turned up an address for Kate, so he'd decided to search the Talavera house for information. Picking the lock on the front door hadn't been a problem, but the last person he'd expected to find inside was Kate.

Especially since she was nothing like he remembered.

When had she turned from a sweet, chubby kid with a crooked smile into a sweet, sexy woman with a luscious mouth that could drive a man wild? Not to mention her big brown eyes, generous curves and legs that went on forever and a day.

The sight of her had turned him from a coolheaded professional into a man who could barely think straight. He'd almost blown the mission and now found himself in deeper than he ever wanted to be.

It was time for a new strategy.

Kate conferred with a clerk at the front desk, then turned to face him. "Looks like we're full tonight, but there should be a room opening up tomorrow. So I guess that means you'll have to stay with me."

His pulse picked up a notch at the implied invitation. *Business, Gannon,* he reminded himself sternly. *Keep your mind on the mission.* He took a deep breath. "Are you sure that won't be too much trouble?"

She smiled. "Not at all. I'm in one of the employee suites, so there's plenty of room."

It was a perfect setup. He'd be in the same room

with the skirt. As soon as Kate was asleep tonight, he could grab it, then hop on the first airplane out of Seattle. Except...

She would know he was the one who stole it.

Usually Brock didn't give a damn about what people thought of him. But somehow the idea of her believing he was a thief, as well as a liar, unsettled him. When he thought of Kate telling the rest of the Talaveras the story, his blood turned cold.

But what choice did he have? If he didn't take the skirt, someone else would.

He followed Kate to the elevator, which took them to her third-floor suite. The door opened to a tasteful sitting area with a computer desk and fax machine in one corner. A small kitchenette graced the other corner of the room, complete with small refrigerator, microwave, hot plate and sink. Another door led to a bedroom in the back and a luxurious bathroom lay in between.

"This is nice," he said, setting his suitcase next to the door.

"It's been home for the past couple of months. We've been so busy at the hotel, that I'm working most of the time anyway, so it's handy."

He folded his arms across his chest. "Where do you want me to sleep?"

To his surprise, he saw a pretty pink blush steal up her neck and settle in her cheeks. Was it possible that he wasn't the only one having erotic fantasies about that king-size bed in the next room?

"On the sofa. It might be a little lumpy, but it should be long enough for you. I can have some extra linens and pillows sent up."

"Sounds good." Not as good as sharing a pillow with Kate, but a man couldn't have everything.

She glanced at the computer. "Do you mind if I check my e-mail, or do you want to go straight to bed?"

"I think I'll hop in the shower if you don't mind." He didn't tell her it was going to be a cold one.

"Go right ahead."

Once Kate was alone in the sitting room she phoned housekeeping, then hurried over to the computer desk and sat down. It only took a few moments for the computer to come to life and begin downloading her e-mail.

Most of the messages were related to upcoming conferences and meetings. But two of them made her sit up in her chair. They were both from Todd Winslow. Kate heard the shower running in the bathroom and did her best not to picture Brock standing under the stream of pulsating water. A naked Brock.

She took a deep breath and turned her attention back to the computer, clicking on Todd's first message. The opening line made her smile.

Dear Kate,
It sprinkled here in Los Angeles today and I
thought of you and that lovely Seattle weather.
I'll have to buy an umbrella sometime in the
next two weeks. You wouldn't believe all the
things I have laid out to pack for my trip. It's almost like I'm moving back home. Hey, maybe
that's not such a bad idea.
Fondly,

Todd

It was a typical e-mail from Todd. He made it a
point to e-mail her every day now. Sometimes just to
say hello. Once in awhile he sent along a joke or told
her about a problem he was having at work. Over the
past few weeks, his messages had become more per-
sonal. He'd mentioned several times how anxious he
was to see her again.

Kate just hoped he had the same reaction as Brock
when he saw her in the skirt. Just thinking about that
flare of heat she'd seen in Brock's gray eyes made her
heart skip a beat. If the skirt could affect a man as im-
placable as Brock Gannon, it could work on anyone.

She clicked on the next message, surprised that
Todd had broken his routine and sent her two
e-mails on the same day. She was even more surprised when she read it.

Kate,
I'm normally not an impulsive person but it's
late and I've been thinking about you and I'm
going to ask you before I chicken out. Will you
go out to dinner with me when I get to Seattle?
Hopefully yours,

Todd

Kate stared at the computer screen, unable to believe her eyes. He'd asked her out. Todd Winslow.
High school golden boy. Owner of one of the most
successful home shopping networks on cable television. She planted both palms on the computer desk
and took a deep breath. It was happening. It was really happening.

And he hadn't even seen her in the skirt yet!

Once he did…anything could happen. Chelsea and
Gwen were proof of that. In a few short weeks, it
could be Kate walking down the aisle. She closed her
eyes, picturing the moment. The glow of happiness
on her bridegroom's face. Her eyes flew open when
she realized the man waiting at the altar in her imag-
ination was not Todd Winslow.

It was Brock Gannon.

Flustered, she stood up at the same time a soft
knock sounded on the door to her suite. She let the
housekeeper in, then helped her make up the sofa.
There was a perfectly logical explanation for confus-

ing Brock with Todd, she thought to herself as she plumped a feather pillow. She hadn't seen Todd in person for over a decade, just his image on television.

While Brock was in the next room. *Naked* in the next room. And she had to admit he'd turned into a strikingly handsome man. Okay, handsome might be an understatement. Just looking at him made her long for steamy nights and silk sheets. But any woman would be having fantasies about him. It was perfectly natural.

"Will there be anything else, Ms. Talavera?" the maid asked.

"No, thank you, Marva," Kate replied, handing her a tip. "Wait a minute, there is one more thing." She walked into the bedroom and pulled the skirt out of the closet. "Could you make sure this gets to the drycleaner for me? It has a small spot near the hem and I'm afraid to wash it."

"Certainly," Marva said, taking the hanger out of Kate's hand. "It should be back on Friday."

"I'm going to call the drycleaner tomorrow morning and give him special instructions, so I'll probably make arrangements to pick it up myself."

"Very well, Ms. Talavera."

As soon as the maid left the suite, Kate marched over to the computer and sat down to accept Todd's invitation. This was not a time for second thoughts. Not when her dream was about to come true.

She knew Todd was perfect for her. He was bright, articulate and successful. They'd practically grown up together. Not that she'd spent a lot of time with Todd back then, since they had run with different crowds. In fact, more than once she'd gotten the feeling that he went out of his way to avoid her. But she'd probably just been paranoid about her weight. Besides, they were both older now. More mature. She'd dated enough Mr. Wrongs to know a Mr. Right when she saw one.

Although, she hadn't actually seen him, except on his television show. And she'd only recently begun corresponding with him. Seeing Brock again reminded her how much a person could change. He definitely didn't seem like the same recalcitrant boy who had been in detention as regularly as he'd raided their refrigerator.

Kate smiled to herself, remembering how intrigued she'd once been by him. At fourteen, she'd just discovered gothic romances and in her mind, seventeen year old Brock Gannon had embodied the perfect gothic hero. Dark. Brooding. A little dangerous.

There was still an aura of danger around him, although it didn't scare her. Just the opposite, in fact. Brock Gannon exuded a primal sensuality that was both daunting and exciting. It was in his stormy gray eyes and the set of his square jaw. The way he carried himself, with a cool confidence that made other men seem insignificant in comparison. Kate couldn't deny that she found him fascinating.

"What am I doing?" she muttered to herself when she realized she was thinking about Brock again. Focusing her attention back on the computer screen, she hit the send button before she had time to talk herself out of it. Todd Winslow was the right man for her.

He had to be.

The sound of the bathroom door opening made her turn around in the chair. Brock emerged, wearing only a pair of plaid cotton pajama pants tied low on his waist with a drawstring. The dark hair on his chest still glistened with tiny droplets of water. The scent of soap and male permeated the air. His short hair was slicked back on his head and his feet were bare.

"I didn't mean to interrupt you," he said, moving toward the sofa.

"No, I'm all finished here." She stood up, her mouth suddenly dry. Okay, so maybe Brock did have solid broad shoulders, a tight washboard stomach and bulging muscles in his arms. It's not like she'd never seen a man's naked body before. Maybe none quite as spectacular as Brock's, but with all the same basic parts. Images of those parts flashed in her mind, sending a wave of heat through her.

She watched as he pulled back the blanket on the sofa bed, then lay down and settled back against the pillow. He pulled the sheet up to his waist so that all she could see was his bare chest. It gave the illusion that he wasn't wearing anything. His flat nipples were a dusky pink and the cords of his neck stood out as he folded his hands behind his head.

She swallowed. "How was the shower?"

He hesitated. "Refreshing."

Kate turned and switched the computer off. Maybe sharing a hotel suite with Brock wasn't such a great idea after all. It put all sorts of crazy notions in her head. "I think I'll go to bed. It's been an exhausting day."

"Good night, Kate."

"Good night." She practically ran for the bedroom. Closing the door behind her, she leaned against it and took a deep breath. Then another. Why did Brock Gannon have to show up in her life again? Why did he have to make her start doubting the perfect future she had all planned out for herself?

"Two weeks," she said softly, slipping out of her pantsuit and hanging it in the closet. Then she took her favorite nightshirt out of the dresser drawer. It was a man's striped pajama top that hung three inches above her knees.

She pulled back the quilted comforter and climbed

into bed. "In two weeks, Brock will be gone and I'll forget all about him."

If she was lucky, in two weeks she'd be planning a wedding. *Mrs. Todd Winslow.* It had a nice ring to it. But when she closed her eyes, she still saw Brock Gannon standing at the altar.

BROCK WINCED as he turned the doorknob leading to the bedroom. He hoped the slight squeak hadn't awakened Kate. Moving stealthily into the room, he paused until his eyes adjusted to the darkness. After a few moments, he could make out Kate's long slender form on the bed. He could hear the steady rhythm of her soft breathing. See the shadows of her silky curls spilling over the pillow. She lay on her side, both hands tucked under one cheek. Her pink lips slightly parted—looking so very kissable.

He turned toward the closet before he forgot the reason he'd come in here. It was time to get the skirt and get the hell out of Kate's life. Putting over three thousand miles between the two of them would be better than a cold shower. At least, he hoped so.

Brock padded silently to the closet, then slowly pulled open the accordion door. He quickly sifted through the row of dresses and pantsuits hanging there, searching for the skirt. He froze when he heard Kate roll over in bed, a soft, breathy sigh escaping her lips. The sound made his body instantly harden.

It was a sound a woman made when he touched her in just the right place.

A sweat broke out on his forehead as he turned back to the closet. Where the hell was that skirt? He sorted through the clothes again, more carefully this time. At last he stepped back and closed the closet door. It wasn't there. Hell.

He turned to look at Kate, wondering if she'd hidden it. But where? At that moment, she opened her eyes, then gasped aloud when she saw him. She bolted upright in bed, struggling with the tangled bedcovers.

"It's all right," he whispered, realizing this was the second time he'd scared her in less than twenty-four hours and hating himself for it.

"Brock." Her voice was husky from sleep. She twisted to switch on the table lamp. Light flooded the room, making them both wince at the brightness. "What are you doing in my bedroom?"

"I heard you cry out," he improvised, moving closer to the bed. "I thought you might be having a nightmare."

"Oh." Another blush suffused her cheeks and she didn't quite meet his eyes. "No, it wasn't a nightmare. It was just a dream."

Torture. That was the word for this mission. Kate lay in bed, not two feet away from him. Her hair was tousled and her cheeks rosy. Her tongue darted out to moisten her lips. His entire body throbbed.

Brock sat down beside her on the bed to conceal his uncomfortable, and no doubt visible, condition. He reached out one hand and tipped up her chin with his finger. "Are you sure?"

She stared into his eyes, then licked her lips. "Positive."

"I'm glad," he said huskily, then he leaned forward, unable to help himself. He was already in this far. And a man could only take so much temptation. He closed the distance between them until his lips met hers.

She tasted even better than he had imagined. Like a spring rain on the parched earth of his soul. His hands found her waist as he deepened the kiss, nipping lightly at her lower lip. She made that sound again, that soft sigh that instantly sent his body into high alert.

At last she pulled back and stared at him, her beautiful brown eyes wide and confused. "I don't think this is a good idea."

He completely agreed, but asked the question anyway. "Why not?"

"I'm involved with someone," she said, then cleared her throat. "Sort of involved. I don't want any complications in my life right now."

"The man you told your parents about," he

guessed. "The one who is supposed to see you in that skirt."

She nodded. "I think he's the one."

Brock wanted to change her mind. And he knew a dozen ways to do it. Ways that could bring them both to the pinnacle of satisfaction. Ways that could induce her to tell him anything he wanted to know. But something made him pull back. A nagging sense of integrity that he'd never let affect his work before.

He straightened and stepped away from the bed. "Then I'll say good night."

"Good night, Brock."

He walked out of the room, closing the door behind him. He wanted the skirt. He wanted Kate. But he didn't have his hands on the former and couldn't have his hands on the latter. This mission was becoming more complicated by the moment.

He headed into the bathroom for a second cold shower.

4

THE NEXT DAY, Kate sat in the back seat of the taxi, her appointment calendar open on her lap. She'd just come from the Sweet Tooth Bakery, where she'd selected a six-layer cake for her parents' anniversary party. She crossed that item off the list, then swallowed a groan at the endless errands she had left to do.

The taxi turned a sharp corner and Kate swayed in her seat, along with the black skirt hanging in the dry cleaner's bag on the window opposite her. Her stomach churned when she thought of the next time she'd wear it. Her date with Todd. The man who might very well be the father of her children.

She reached into her purse for a roll of antacids, wishing she hadn't eaten quite so many cake samples at the bakery. She'd finally chosen the raspberry chocolate flavor with white chocolate cream frosting. It was both delicious and decadent.

While she was there, she couldn't help but look at their wedding cake catalog. The bakery needed at least two weeks' notice on all wedding cake orders, so she'd have to take that into consideration when she and Todd set the date for their wedding. She hoped he was one of those people who liked short engagements. Kate wanted the deed done before either one of them had time for second thoughts.

The taxi squealed to a stop in front of the hotel.

"Five dollars even," the cabbie said, tipping up his worn denim cap.

A knock on the taxi window made her look up from her purse. Brock Gannon stood right outside. He wore dark sunglasses in deference to the bright, Seattle sky. When he smiled at her, a dimple flashing in his cheek, every rational thought fled from her head.

He opened her car door. "I've been waiting for you."

"Brock." She swallowed, tasting the minty flavor of the antacid on her dry tongue. "What are you doing here?"

"I came to take you out for lunch."

She reached for her appointment calendar. "Did we have a date?" Heat crawled up her cheeks at the slip of the tongue. She would have remembered if Brock had asked her for a date. "I mean, an appointment?"

"Five dollars," the cabbie reminded her, a tinge of irritation in his voice.

"Oh, right," Kate said, peeling off a tip from the

pile of crumpled dollar bills in her hand. Her purse fell off her lap, the contents spilling onto the dirty cab floor.

As she scrambled to stuff everything back inside, Brock slid his wallet out of his back pocket and handed the cabbie a five, along with a two dollar tip, which was much more generous than she'd intended to be, given the unnecessarily bumpy cab ride. In her job, she'd learned to value good customer service.

She climbed out of the cab, her heart beating wildly in her chest. It was the surprise of seeing Brock again, she told herself, as the cab peeled away from the curb. And the fact that he'd changed so much. Today he was wearing snug denim jeans and a black polo shirt that made a woman think of pleasure instead of business. She still wasn't used to the way his lanky teenage body had evolved into bulging muscles that kept drawing her attention to his arms, chest and shoulders. Her gaze moved lower. He filled out those jeans quite nicely, too.

"Kate?"

She jerked up her head, realizing she'd been admiring that region a little too long. The half grin on his face told her he'd noticed her attention. Not that she was about to admit it. "Yes?"

"Are you hungry?"

For some reason, those three innocent words took on a whole new meaning. She'd been attracted to men before, but never experienced anything quite like this. There had to be a reasonable explanation for it.

"I thought we could go to the deli across the street," Brock said, when she didn't reply to his question. "Unless you have a better suggestion."

Kate met his gaze, telling herself to snap out of it. "I already had some cake."

He smiled. "That sounds nutritious."

The way he looked at her made her breath catch in her throat. "It had raspberries in it. Fruit is good for you. Very healthy."

"You do look healthy," he agreed, his gaze lingering down the length of her body. "Incredible, in fact."

She could see the flare of desire in his eyes and marveled at it. Especially since she wasn't even wearing the skirt.

The skirt.

Kate looked down at her hands, which held only her purse and leather-bound appointment book, then whirled around hoping to see the dry cleaner bag on the sidewalk behind her. "Oh, no!"

"Is something wrong?" he asked.

"Wrong?" she echoed, her stomach twisting into a tight knot. "Wrong? Yes, something's wrong. That taxi just took off with my skirt!"

"But you're wearing pants today," he said, his gaze dropping below her neck once again.

Kate looked down at her simple cobalt blue pant-suit, wondering what Brock found so fascinating about it. But she didn't have time to figure it out. The skirt was gone. And she had to find it. Her entire future depended on it.

"I just picked up my skirt at the drycleaners. The skirt that's going to change my life!" She headed for the pay phone on the corner. She didn't want to waste time by going to her office on the fifth floor of the hotel.

Understanding dawned on his face. He dug in his pocket for a quarter. "It was a Happy Days cab, right?"

"I think so." She walked into the telephone booth, still baffled by the fact that she'd let that cab drive away with her skirt still inside.

Brock stepped in beside her, picking up the telephone directory dangling by a wire cable beneath the phone. "I'll look up the number."

"Thanks," she replied, inhaling the musky scent of his aftershave. The phone booth was small and Brock was large, so their bodies brushed together. Once. Twice. A warmth spread from deep inside her belly to all four limbs, making her fingers shake a little as she dropped the quarter into the coin slot of the pay phone.

He flipped through the yellow pages. "Here's the number—555-8989."

She punched the buttons on the dial pad, all too aware of how close Brock stood to her. One more step and he'd have her backed against the wall of the phone booth. That thought made the warmth inside of her turn into a liquid heat. She turned away from him as the line began to ring, trying to gather her thoughts.

"Happy Days," a man answered after the tenth ring.

"My name is Kate Talavera," she began, twisting the wire phone cord between her fingers, "and I just took a ride in one of your cabs."

"Sorry, lady," he replied, "All complaints must be made in writing."

"No, wait!" she cried before he hung up. "I'm not calling to complain. I left something in the cab."

"Not a problem," the man said. "Can you tell me your drop-off location?"

"I'm at the corner of Yesler Way and Madison."

"Let me put you on hold while I check the log."

Kate tapped her foot as canned music drifted over the line.

"Well?" Brock asked, his breath fanning her cheek. "What did he say?"

"He's checking," she replied, suddenly aware of

how warm it was in the booth. The Plexiglas walls were beginning to steam up.

The dispatcher came back on the line. "Okay, you were in Archie's cab, number 513. Can you describe the item you lost?"

"It's a skirt. A very special skirt."

"We'll need an exact description."

"It's black, with a shiny black thread running through it," she said, wondering how many abandoned black skirts there could be in Happy Days cabs. "And it's in a drycleaner's bag. Lemburg Drycleaners."

"Let me radio Archie and tell him," the dispatcher said, putting her on hold once more.

"You forgot to mention that the skirt is sexy as hell," Brock breathed in her hair. "Or maybe I should say, you in the skirt."

She turned and found him so close that the front of her jacket brushed against his shirt. For the first time she realized that she barely reached his chin. It was an odd, overpowering feeling. She searched for something to say. "You've grown, Brock."

He smiled. "I'd say we've both changed a lot in the last twelve years."

He'd certainly never looked at her like this when she was fifteen. But then, Brock and her brother had been too busy chasing after girls their own age. Or rather, letting girls chase them. And more often than not, letting themselves be caught. She could only imagine how many women Brock had met when he'd joined the Navy. No doubt leaving a string of broken hearts around the world.

"So is your skirt there?" Brock asked, reaching out to straighten her lapel. His fingers were so close to her breast that it began to tingle.

She placed her palm over the mouthpiece, pretending his nearness didn't affect her. "He's contacting the taxi cab driver."

Brock braced his hand on the clear Plexiglass wall above her head and leaned in even closer. "You smell terrific."

"It's a new perfume," she breathed, her knees turning mushy.

"I like it. What's it called?"

She licked her lips, then watched his gaze fall to her mouth. "Seduction."

He moved slightly and Kate was certain he was going to kiss her. She held her breath, then heard the gravelly voice of the dispatcher in her ear once again. Brock must have been close enough to hear it, too, because he drew back. She took a deep breath and forced her mind to focus on the conversation.

"Archie's not answering his radio," the dispatcher said, as a loud horn honked in the background. "He's probably taking a bathroom break. The guy's got some real serious prostate problems. Seems like he's always making a trip to the john."

This was more information than she needed to know. "What exactly is the procedure when someone leaves something in one of your cabs?"

"The drivers are required to turn any items into our lost and found department."

"Right away? I mean, is it possible he's still driving around with my skirt?"

"Sure. He probably hasn't even noticed it in there yet. I remember one time some lady left her baby sleeping in the back seat of my cab. I drove around for an hour before it woke up and started hollering. Didn't even know it was there. Can you believe none of my fares ever said a word about it? And then another time..."

"I'm in a bit of a hurry," Kate interjected, before he could launch into another story. "Can you radio him again? This is very important to me."

"His shift is due to end soon, so he should be coming in any minute. If you want to stop by here, you can pick up your skirt."

"I'm on my way." She hung up the phone, then turned around and bumped right into Brock, who still stood in the phone booth. He reached out to steady her, his big hands gripping her waist.

"You're going to the cab company?"

She nodded, much too aware of the strength of his

hold on her. The warmth of his broad fingers. "The cab should be back by the time I get there."

"I'll give you a ride."

She took a deep breath, wishing he'd let go of her. Wishing he'd pull her closer. "That's not necessary."

"I insist," he said, finally stepping away from her. "It's my fault you left the skirt in the cab. I distracted you."

That was an understatement. She gave a shaky nod of assent, not really wanting to retrieve her own car from the hotel's parking garage. She followed him out of the phone booth to the curb where his car was parked, her skin still tingling from the touch of his hands.

He opened the car door for her. Brock had leased a brand new silver Camaro convertible, almost the same color as his eyes. It had gray leather interior. She slid into the butter-soft seat, then unspooled the seat belt as Brock circled around the front of the car.

"Are you sure you don't mind giving me a ride?" she asked, as he slid into the driver's seat next to her.

He gave her another heart-stopping smile. "I can't think of anything I'd rather do."

5

BROCK AND KATE ran the three blocks from their parking space to the Happy Days cab company, the rain soaking them both to the skin. Brock raked his wet hair off his forehead as they stepped through the door. The musty air inside the old building wasn't much better, but at least it was dry.

"This just isn't my day," Kate said, patting down her wet curls. "First I lose my skirt, and now my pantsuit is ruined."

Brock's gaze fell to the silky front of her pantsuit where the wet fabric molded to her breasts. He forgot about the rain and the musty air and his mission to find the skirt as he took a step closer to her. A low, appreciative whistle made him look up. He saw several men loitering by a row of vending machines and ogling Kate.

"Here," he said gruffly, shrugging out of his jacket. "Put this on. I can't believe you left the hotel without a coat. Even if it is over fifty degrees out today."

"I'm not cold," she replied, still finger combing her hair.

"Parts of you obviously are."

She looked down at her chest and her cheeks flooded. Grabbing the jacket out of his hands, she pulled it on, then hugged the lapels close to her chest. "Thank you."

"Don't mention it."

He followed her to the dispatch desk, trying not to think of how she looked in that pantsuit. Or how she would look out of it. He didn't have time for a fling. Besides, Kate wasn't that kind of girl. At least, she wasn't twelve years ago. Back then, she'd been shy. A little chubby. Always disappearing into her room whenever he stopped by the Talavera house. She'd changed a lot since then.

But had he?

Brock's career was almost as shady as his past. And what did he really have to offer a woman like Kate, other than a hot one-night stand? She was from a good family with strong roots. He was like a tumbleweed just blowing through town.

But what if she wanted him as much as he wanted her?

He shook his head, clearing it of the impending fantasy. She'd made her feelings crystal clear last night. *This isn't a good idea.* Maybe he should write it down to remind himself when other parts of his body started doing his thinking for him.

Kate walked up to the desk. "I'm Kate Talavera," she told the dispatcher. "I just called regarding a skirt I left in one of your cabs."

"Right," the dispatcher said, hitching his thumb behind him. "Archie came in a few minutes ago. He's in the manager's office. Mad as hell, too."

"Why?" Brock asked, a sinking feeling in his gut.

"Sorry, that's company business. I can take your number and have him give you a call."

"We'd rather talk to him now." Brock headed for the office door before the dispatcher could argue with him.

Kate followed him, still holding his jacket firmly around her. "Maybe they're firing him. He didn't have the best driving skills."

"I hope it's that simple," Brock said, then opened the door without knocking.

The cabbie sat alone in the office, holding an ice pack on the back of his head. He looked up as they walked in. "Can you believe this crap? What kind of world do we live in when old ladies go around mugging people?"

"You were mugged?" Kate exclaimed.

"She bashed me right in the noggin with her purse. Must have had an anvil in it. Then she cleaned out my cab. Took everything. The money, the seat cover, the flashlight I keep in the glove compartment. Even a damn map of the city. How desperate can people get?"

"My skirt." Kate asked, taking a step closer to him. "Did she take my skirt?"

Archie slouched down in his chair. "Yeah. She took everything. Lucky I use a strong adhesive on my toupee or she probably would have taken that, too!"

Kate's shoulders slumped. "I don't believe this."

"Believe it, lady. The streets aren't safe for nobody no more. Imagine a sweet little old granny going around mugging innocent people. It just ain't right."

"Do you remember what she looks like?" Brock asked.

"'Course I remember." Archie winced as he shifted the ice pack on his head. "She was a chubby thing with twinkling blue eyes. Looked like Mrs. Santa Claus. Innocent as could be. Even wore bifocals. That's why she caught me off guard."

"Did she say anything?" Kate asked.

"Naw. Didn't want to make small talk. Just hopped in my cab at the corner of Madison and Tenth Avenue and told me to drive her to Myrtle Street, I'd barely pulled up to the curb when she whacked me with her purse. Hurt like hell, too."

"Maybe you should see a doctor," Kate suggested.

"Not until I talk to the cops. They're on their way.

'Course they never seem to be in any hurry, unless they're headed for a donut shop."

"Can we take a look at your cab?" Brock asked.

"Sure," the cabbie replied. "It's parked in the back of the garage. Number 513. But I'm telling you the skirt ain't there. She took everything. I'll tell you—" Archie reached up to adjust his toupee "—it's a sad day in the world when a mugger steals a man's hat off of his head."

Kate dug in her purse, then pulled out a business card. "Will you please call me if you get any information about the thief? It's very important."

"That skirt must really mean a lot to you," Archie mused as he took her card. "I've had my cap for twenty years and it's still as good as new. Probably won't be able to drive the same without it."

"Thank you for your help," Kate said, then followed Brock out of the office.

"Now what?" She sighed. "Should I make a police report?"

"I think we'll get farther investigating this on our own." He headed toward the back of the garage, spotting cab number 513 near an overhead door.

"Wait a minute, Brock. What do you mean we? This isn't your problem."

He turned to face her. "Do you think I'm really going to let you try to track down a dangerous mugger by yourself?"

"She's an old lady."

"Who gives people concussions with her purse."
He opened the driver's door of the cab and peered
inside.

"You probably shouldn't touch anything," Kate
warned. "The police will want to check for fingerprints."

Brock leaned over the bench seat to look in the
back of the cab. "There's no way the police would be
able to differentiate the prints of the mugger from the
hundreds of other fares who have ridden in this cab.
Including yours."

"I suppose you're right."

He turned and looked at her over his shoulder.
"How clean was the cab when you rode in it?"

"The floor was dirty. Just lots of gravel and grit.
Why?"

"Because I think we may have found our first
clue." He climbed out of the front seat and opened
the back door, then pointed to a foam cup laying
crumpled on the floor. "Was this on the floor?"

The words Perk Up Cafe were printed on the side
of the cup.

"I didn't notice it when I dropped my purse."

"Is there a coffeehouse on the corner of Madison
and Tenth Avenue?"

Her brown eyes widened. "Yes. Right on the corner."

He grinned. "Guess where I'm taking you for lunch."

KATE TOOK a bite of her tuna salad sandwich, the aroma of the chocolate amaretto coffee in front of her teasing her nostrils. "This is wonderful."

"At least our mugger has good taste," Brock said, before taking a man-size bite out of his Philly cheese-steak sandwich.

She sighed. "I just wish the trail hadn't run dry. The manager swears he hasn't seen anyone matching her description."

"Are you ready to give up?" Brock asked.

She shook her head. "Not on your life. I'm not stopping until I find the skirt."

He wiped his mouth with a paper napkin, then leaned back in his chair. "Don't you think it's about time you told me a little more about this skirt? Exactly why is it so important to you?"

Kate placed her sandwich on her paper plate, then licked a drop of mayonnaise off her thumb. She'd been expecting him to ask about it. Pulling his coat around her, she savored its warmth and the subtle scent of Brock that wafted from it. Why did her plan to seduce Todd with the skirt suddenly seem so ridiculous?

"You don't have to tell me," Brock said as the silence stretched between them.

"No, I'm sure you must be wondering what all the fuss is about."

"I think I already know. I was hiding under your bed the other night, remember?"

How could she possibly forget? "I suppose you think it's silly to believe that a skirt can win a man's love?"

"Yes."

She sat forward in her chair and pushed her plate away. "Well, if you'd seen what happened to Torrie, Chelsea and Gwen, you'd be a believer."

"Who are Torrie, Chelsea and Gwen?"

"My best friends from college. They each wore the skirt, then *Bam!*" She snapped her fingers. "They each found the love of their life."

"Sounds like coincidence to me. Or more likely, the power of positive thinking. They each expected to find a man when they wore the skirt, so they did."

"Please. It's not that simple to find an eligible single male anymore. Believe me, I know."

His gaze made her go hot all over. "Maybe you just haven't been looking in the right places."

"Maybe. The point is, I think I've finally found the right one. I just want the skirt to seal the bargain."

"Bargain?" He arched a brow. "That sounds romantic."

She smiled. "Well, bargains are this man's specialty. He owns a very successful retail business."

Brock didn't look impressed. Which only reinforced her decision not to tell him the name of her Mr. Right. He might still be bitter about the fact that Todd Winslow was the reason he'd been expelled from high school. Especially since Todd apparently hadn't suffered any consequences from their fight. He'd stayed in school and gone on to graduate at the top of her class.

"I guess it's your life," he said at last.

"Exactly. That's why I'm perfectly capable of tracking down the skirt myself."

He shook his head. "No. I told you I would help and I'm a man of my word." Brock tossed his napkin on his empty plate, then waved the waiter over to the table. "We're ready for the check."

"Certainly, sir." The waiter shuffled through the bills in his leather apron, then pulled one out. "Will there be anything else?"

"Yes," Brock replied, opening his wallet. "A very generous tip if you can give us some information."

The waiter glanced toward the manager at the cash register, then took a step closer to the table. "What kind of information?"

Brock set a hundred dollar bill on the table. "We're looking for one of your customers. I don't know if she's a regular, but she was in here earlier today and bought a cup of coffee to go."

The waiter looked mournfully at the Ben Franklin

on the table. "We get dozens of customers every hour."

"This one was an older lady. Wore bifocals. Looks like Mrs. Santa Claus."

A smile broke over the waiter's face. "Oh, yeah, her I definitely remember. She ordered a double espresso and a bran muffin."

"Do you know her name?"

The waiter shook his head. "No, but she comes in every Tuesday and Thursday about noon and places an order to go. Lots of the players do."

"Players?" Kate echoed, looking from the waiter to Brock and back again.

"Bingo players," the waiter explained. "There's a bingo hall right down the street. They have senior citizen discount bingo twice a week. It attracts a lot of the older crowd."

"And you think that's where this lady was coming from?"

The waiter nodded. "She was wearing a Steelhead Bingo Hall T-shirt, if that tells you anything."

"Thanks," Brock said, pushing the one hundred dollar bill across the table to the waiter. "You've been a big help."

Kate stared at Brock as the waiter cleared their plates, then walked away. "I don't believe it."

He flashed a smile. "It's amazing what you can discover if you talk to the right people."

"No. I don't believe you just spent a hundred dollars to find my skirt. Next time, could you start out with a twenty and work your way up?" She opened her purse. "I don't carry that kind of cash around with me. I'll have to write you a check."

"Forget it," he said, rising out of his chair.

"I can't just forget it," she said, following him out of the coffeehouse. "I owe you. I'm searching for a skirt to help me win the man of my dreams and you just spent a hundred dollars to help me do it. I want to know why."

Once they were out on the sidewalk, he turned to face her. "Are you sure you want to know the reason?"

His face was so intense on her that she swallowed. "Yes. I'm sure."

He took a step closer to her, reaching one hand out to gently brush a stray tendril of hair off her cheek. "Because I can't seem to help myself."

Kate blinked. Then she understood. It was the skirt. He'd seen her wearing it the other night and it was obviously still affecting him. She tried to ignore the stab of disappointment deep inside of her that his attraction wasn't genuine.

She took a deep breath. "Then there's only one thing to do."

His hand still lingered near her hair. He trailed one finger down the length of her cheek, the sensation causing goose bumps to erupt over her entire body. "What?"

She took a deep breath as a hundred erotic images crowded her mind. "Go to the bingo hall."

6

BROCK PULLED another one hundred dollar bill out of his wallet and held it out to the custodian at the bingo hall. "Maybe this can refresh your memory."

The custodian's face lit up as she reached for the bill. "You know, I do seem to remember a woman who looks like Mrs. Santa Claus. Plump, with white hair and bifocals. Always plays ten cards at a time. Takes real skill to do that."

The woman reached for the bill, but Brock held it out of her reach. "We need a name."

The woman's forehead wrinkled as she searched her memory. "Clarks...no, Clarkson. Petula Clarkson. That's the name she uses when she signs in every week. I remember because Petula Clark was one of my husband's favorite singers. I preferred Perry Como myself."

Brock's pulse picked up a notch. Were they finally closing in on the skirt? "I don't suppose you have her phone number or address handy?"

The woman shook her head. "No, but how many Petula Clarkson's can there be in the city?"

Twenty minutes later, Kate and Brock discovered the answer to that question.

"There are ten people listed as P. Clarkson." Brock tore the page out of the directory, then stepped away from the telephone booth.

Kate stood by his car. "Ten? Where do we start?"

"At the beginning." They both got in the car, then he flipped open his cell phone and dialed the telephone number at the top of the list of P. Clarksons.

"May I speak with Petula, please?" He hesitated a moment. "Okay, thank you."

"No Petula?"

"No Petula." He looked at the directory page, then punched out the number on his cell phone. "Nine more to go."

Kate sat in the passenger seat, caressing the soft seat cushion. "I never asked what you do for a living."

He glanced over at her. "I'm in the salvage business."

Salvage? How did a man who dealt in salvage every day afford a car like this?

"Sorry, wrong number," Brock said into the phone, then dialed the next number.

She studied him as he punched the buttons on his cell phone. Brock was almost as uncommunicative now as he had been as a teenager. He never volunteered any information about himself, although he seemed oddly curious about her life. Still, there was no denying that he was an incredibly attractive man. Her gaze moved to his powerful hands, one holding the phone, the other wrapped around the steering wheel. The broad, blunt-tipped fingers made her yearn to be touched. She closed her eyes, trying to block out the irresistible pull he seemed to have on her.

But it didn't help. His appeal went beyond the mere physical. There was a strength about Brock, a rugged sturdiness that you didn't see much in men anymore. He wasn't afraid to be himself—to go after what he wanted. She'd seen that herself today when he'd gotten information from the cabbie, the waiter and the bingo hall custodian. It was more than his money that made them talk. It was the air of command about him.

Which didn't fit with a man who worked in the salvage business. Just like the car didn't fit.

"Who are you really?" she asked, after he'd dialed another number.

Brock slowly turned and stared at her. "What do you mean? You know who I am."

The sudden tension inside the car was palpable. Kate knew her instincts had been right. "You're not in the salvage business. I can't see you selling junk car parts to people."

He gave her a wry smile. "I guess I'll never make a good salesman if I can't even sell you on the idea."

She arched a brow. "Why should you have to sell me? Why don't you just tell me the truth?"

He hesitated, then closed his phone and turned toward her. "Because my line of work isn't something I like to talk about, Kate. I'm a private person."

"You can't even tell me?"

He shifted away from her and stared out the window. "I'm a mercenary."

She stared at him, her entire body growing tense. "A gun for hire?"

He shook his head. "No, I don't kill people. But I am for hire. Mostly to recover stolen goods when someone wants a job done that's a little...messy, they contact the agency I work for and I take care of it for them."

Her shoulders relaxed. "It doesn't sound exactly legal."

"Most of the time it is. Although, occasionally I have to cut corners to get the job done."

She considered his words. "So that's why you're so good at prying information out of people. You do it for a living."

"I may be good, but I'm tired of it, Kate. It's...lonely."

"So do something else."

He sighed. "Like what?"

She reached out her hand without thinking and laid it on his bare forearm. His skin was warm. She heard him inhale sharply as her fingers trickled through the silky hair on his arms and caressed the sinewy muscle. ''Work for me.''

He turned toward her, his gray eyes molten with desire. ''I can think of other things I'd rather do at the moment.''

She opened her mouth, but he closed the distance between them before she could speak. His lips molded against her own, a low moan rumbling in his chest. Her hands gripped his shoulders as his mouth moved over hers. Savoring. Seeking. Then he stopped just as suddenly and pulled back.

''I'm sorry.'' He raked one hand through his hair. ''Hell, I don't know what came over me. You told me last night that this wasn't a good idea. I need to respect that.''

Kate struggled to sit up and gather her scattered wits. ''It's all right, Brock. It's not your fault.''

He took slow, deep breaths, both hands gripping the steering wheel so tightly that his knuckles were white. ''It's not all right. I'm not in the habit of attacking unwilling women, Kate. And I don't intend to start now.''

She cleared her throat, realizing she wasn't exactly unwilling. In fact, she'd been disappointed when he'd stopped kissing her. Somewhere along the line she'd lost all perspective. It was the stress of losing the skirt. That, and the enigma sitting beside her. He'd been honest with her about his line of work. The least she could do was return the favor.

"I'm serious, Brock. It's not your fault. There's a simple explanation for all of this. The skirt has a powerful effect on men. You saw me in it yesterday and are obviously still experiencing a reaction."

He turned to her, a crease in his brow. "Are you completely nuts? No skirt could make me feel this way."

"You said yourself that you've never acted like this before. What other explanation is there?"

He stared at her for two long beats. "Maybe you're right. Maybe it is the skirt."

She nodded, though his admission made her stomach sink. "Of course I'm right. I'm sure if we just ignore it, the reaction will go away sooner or later."

"How do you suggest we do that?"

"By concentrating on work. I was serious about my job offer before. You're already helping me track down the skirt. I'd feel much better if you'd let me pay you for it. I could use some help getting ready for the anniversary party, too. I have a ton of errands left to do and we're busier than ever at the hotel."

"So we're talking short-term employment? Just until the party is over?"

She nodded. "I'd really appreciate the help, Brock.

I've been feeling a little stressed lately. I can't pay much, but..."

"I'll take it," he interjected.

She blinked up at him. "Just like that?"

"Hey, I need the job. And Sid and Rose deserve the best. I've never actually helped throw a party before, but I'm willing to learn as I go."

She smiled, suddenly feeling much better. "Good. It's settled then. You're my new Guy Friday."

"That's right, Kate," he said, his voice growing husky. "Anything you want, all you have to do is ask."

Her gaze fell to his mouth and she knew he wasn't just talking about his new job. But she also knew that his condition was partly her fault. If he hadn't seen her wearing the skirt, he wouldn't be acting this way. Which meant it was up to her to keep things strictly platonic between them.

Even if her hormones were telling her just the opposite.

"The first thing I want you to do," she said, picking up his cell phone off the dash and handing it to him. "Is find Petula."

He took the phone from her, his fingers brushing against her hand and sending a tingle all the way down to her toes.

"Okay," he said, flipping open the phone. "We've

got four down, six to go. We've got to be getting closer."

That's the one thing she was afraid of—getting too close to Brock. Try as she might, she still couldn't forget that heated kiss they'd shared last night. Even knowing his attraction was a direct result of seeing her in the skirt didn't explain *her* attraction to him.

Six phone calls later, Brock wadded up the directory page. "That's it. No Petula."

Her heart sunk. She glanced at her watch, knowing she had to get back to work. "So it's over."

"Not yet."

7

"I FOUND HER."

Kate looked up from her desk to see Brock standing in the doorway. The rest of the offices in her wing of the hotel were dark, her co-workers had all gone home hours ago. She'd been working nonstop ever since Brock had dropped her off at the hotel this afternoon. "Found who?"

"Mrs. Santa Claus." Brock walked into the office, his gaze taking in the chaotic jumble of files on her desk and the overflowing waste basket. "Tough day?"

"You have no idea," she said with a sigh. Then she pushed her chair back from her desk. "But it's definitely getting better. How did you find her?"

He folded his arms across his broad chest. "Trade secret."

Part of her wanted to pry the information out of him, but something in his expression told her she might not want to know. Besides, getting the skirt back was her first priority. "When can we go see her?"

"I telephoned her apartment about twenty minutes ago, but the person who answered told me Petula was already in bed."

"I suppose even muggers need their beauty sleep. Should we call the police?"

"Let's talk to her first," Brock said, perching one hip on her desk. He still wore those tight denim jeans and black polo shirt.

She watched the play of muscles in his forearms, remembering how they'd held her the night before. How warm his breath had felt against her skin. How hungrily his mouth had plundered her own. It was a good thing he'd checked into his own hotel room today. Swallowing hard, she forced her mind back on the subject at hand. "So we'll call first thing tomorrow morning?"

He considered that for a moment. "I think it might be better not to give her any warning. Criminals tend to be a little jumpy. We don't want to scare her off."

"Whatever you say."

"Maybe it would be better if I checked it out on my own tomorrow. These recovery missions can be a little...unpredictable."

"No," She stood up and switched off the adding machine. "I want to be there, too."

She expected him to argue with her, but he just shrugged and said, "Okay. If you're done working tonight, how about joining me for a drink at the bar?"

It was so tempting. That was the problem. It was hard enough to resist Brock when she was sober. One glass of wine and she'd probably forget all about the skirt and Todd and her dream for the future. A dream she was determined to make come true. Besides, she wanted to check her e-mail. There might be another message from Todd waiting for her.

"Can I have raincheck?" she asked, moving toward the door and switching off the overhead light.

"Absolutely." He followed her out of the office and rode with her on the elevator to the third floor. "Why don't you just give me a call tomorrow when you're ready to go see Petula."

"I should be free for an hour or two in the morning," she said, turning down the hallway. Then she stopped short, unable to believe her eyes.

Her father sat in the hotel hallway, his back pressed against the door to her suite and his long legs sprawled out on the floor. He had a small silver flask dangling from one hand.

She was down the hall in a heartbeat. "Dad, what's wrong?"

"Not a thing," Sid Talavera replied. "I just wanted to see my favorite daughter."

"I'm your only daughter." She frowned down at him. "Have you been drinking?"

"Nothing like good, hand-squeezed lemonade to

help you clear away the cobwebs." He held the flask up to her. "See for yourself."

She sniffed and realized he was telling the truth. It *was* lemonade. Her Dad's famous cure for all of life's problems. He used to make it for her whenever she was feeling blue. The Talavera's refrigerator had been well-stocked with lemons during her teen years.

"What's wrong, Dad?"

"Your mother left me." He tipped up the flask and took another deep swig.

Kate mouth fell open. *"Mom left you? That's not possible."*

"I'm afraid it's true, honey." Then his gaze narrowed on the man standing behind her. "Aren't you going to introduce me to your date?"

"This isn't my date," Kate said, her mind whirling. So much for her efforts to keep his arrival a secret. "This is Brock. Brock Gannon."

Sid blinked. "Well, I'll be damned." He stood up, a slow smile spreading across his face. Then he held out one beefy hand. "Brock Gannon. Last time I saw you must have been ten years ago."

"More like twelve." Brock reached out to shake his hand. "Nice to see you again, Sid."

"It's a pleasure," Sid replied, pumping his hand up and down. "A real pleasure. What are you doing back in Seattle? How long have you been here?"

"I just arrived a couple of days ago. Thought I'd pay the place a visit."

Sid skittered a glance toward Kate, then back to Brock. "Really? Is that the only reason or is there something you two want to tell me?"

"No, Dad," Kate assured him. She unlocked her hotel door and swung it open. "It's nothing like that. Brock's staying here at the hotel. We've just been...catching up on old times."

Sid grinned. "Wait until I tell Rosie..." Then his voice faded along with his smile. He sighed. "Guess I won't be telling her anything since she doesn't live with me anymore."

"That's ridiculous." Kate said, ushering him into her suite. "Now sit down and tell me what happened."

Sid set his lemonade flask on the end table, then sank into the sofa. "I already told you, Katie. She left me. Packed up and walked out."

Brock stood in the open doorway. "Maybe I should leave you two alone."

"No," Sid replied, waving him into the room. "Hell, Brock, you're like family. Come on in. I sure don't have anything to hide."

Brock looked at Kate and she gave him a nod. He walked in and closed the door behind him. His presence inexplicably made her feel better. Calmer. As if he could keep her anchored and safe in this sudden storm that had blown up between her parents.

Kate sat down next to her father. "I take it you and Mom had a fight."

"That's right. You were there to witness it."

Her brow furrowed. "When?"

"The other day. Your mother made cannoli for dessert and then lit into me for wanting to enjoy it."

"Define enjoy."

"I ate four of them. Four lousy cannoli. Does that sound like a reason to end a marriage?"

Her blood turned to ice. "Are you two talking about a divorce?"

He grimaced. "Hell, I don't know. Ask your mother."

"I'm asking you."

"I don't want a divorce. But I'm almost sixty years old and if I want to eat five or fifteen or fifty cannoli, I should be able to do it in peace."

"Mom's just worried about you, Dad. You're supposed to be watching your cholesterol and your diet."

He tossed his hands in the air. "Then why did she make the cannoli?"

Kate smiled in sympathy with her father's dilemma. She'd never been able to resist her mother's cooking, either, which is why she'd ballooned to almost two hundred pounds when she was in high school. Moving away from home had proved to be the best diet in the world for her.

"Because she knows how much you like cannoli," Kate replied, "and she wants to make you happy."

"If she wants to make me happy, she should move back home."

"Where did she go?" Brock asked.

"To her sister Flora's house."

Kate breathed a sigh of relief. "Aunt Flora only lives two blocks away from you."

"It's not how far Rose has gone," Sid muttered. "It's the fact that she's gone at all. Hell, I don't know. Maybe it's all for the best."

"You don't mean that," Kate said softly.

Sid jerked up his chin. "The hell I don't. Your mother's not the easiest woman in the world to live with, you know. I'm tired of the nagging. Always telling me what I can eat and what I can't eat. I've had it."

"Dad, be serious. You and Mom love each other."

"Well, I'm not the one who left."

"What makes you think she's not coming back?" Brock asked him.

"Because she packed her suitcase and told me she wasn't coming back," Sid replied. "It was pretty clear. And I'm not about to go begging her to come back, either." He took another swig of lemonade. "A man has his pride."

Kate glanced up at Brock, then back at her father. "Are you sure this is about cannoli?"

"She wants me to retire," Sid announced. "Wants us to buy a yacht and sail around the world. I'm only sixty years old. I have a thriving business. I can't just pick up and leave on a whim."

"I never knew that you two were having problems," Kate said.

"Well, it's been building for a while now." Sid leaned back against the sofa. "Ever since she retired from teaching last year. I think she's going through some kind of midlife crisis."

"You and mom have been together for forty years," Kate said, willing him to listen. "You love her. And I know she loves you."

Sid's shoulders slumped. "I'm not so sure about that anymore."

Her father's despair was contagious. She forgot all about the party. All about the frantic planning of the last few weeks. Were her parents really headed for divorce after all these years?

Brock leaned forward in his chair. "Maybe you both just need some time alone, Sid."

His deep voice soothed the panic welling inside of her. She nodded in agreement. "Brock's right, Dad. This might actually be good for you. Give you both time to think about what you really want."

Sid nodded. "I'll give her all the time she wants. I'm perfectly capable of taking care of myself."

"Dad, you don't even know how to cook."

"Well, that should make your mother happy. She won't have to worry about me eating too much cholesterol."

"Maybe I should come home and take care of you," Kate suggested.

"Absolutely not." Sid's voice was firm. "I won't have you uprooting your life because of this. I'll be all right."

"This can't be happening," Kate muttered under her breath. "I've got to talk to Mom."

Sid stood up. "Give her a few days to cool off. She'll probably be furious with me when she finds out I've talked to you about this. You know how she doesn't like to upset you or Tony."

It was already too late for that. "I am upset, Dad. My parents have separated. Don't you think that's cause for concern?"

Sid hesitated, a stark expression on his face. "I suppose it is. What if she never comes back?"

"Let me take you home, Sid." Brock stood up and pulled his car keys out of his pocket.

"I can walk," Sid replied.

"Walk?" Kate said, incredulous. "Are you telling me you *walked* here? At night? It's over five miles from the house to the hotel!"

He looked sheepish. "I wanted to work off all that cannoli."

"Let Brock take you home," she insisted. "And call me tomorrow."

"You bet, honey." Sid leaned over and kissed his daughter's cheek. "And don't you worry. Everything will be all right. I'm almost sure of it."

A lump rose in her throat as she watched them leave. Her father looked older, smaller, next to Brock. When had his hair turned so gray?

She closed her hotel room door, turning the lock and hooking the chain. An overwhelming urge to call her mother gripped her, but she knew it would be better to wait until tomorrow. She'd be calmer then, and if she was lucky, this marital squall might have blown over.

At least, she hoped so. In less than two weeks, over two hundred guests were attending the Talaveras' fortieth anniversary party. Her brother Tony and his wife Elena were flying in all the way from Brazil. It was supposed to be an evening her parents would never forget.

If they were still together.

"HOW ABOUT a little kick in your lemonade, Brock?" Sid held up a bottle of vodka.

"Thanks, I'm fine." Brock sat in the Talaveras' living room watching a basketball game on the television with the sound muted. Sid had asked him to come in for a nightcap and Brock could tell the older man didn't want to be alone. No doubt he missed his wife.

Sid poured a generous dollop of vodka into his own flask of lemonade, then took a seat in his worn easy chair, the springs groaning in protest at his weight. "So how long do you plan to stay in Seattle?"

Brock shrugged. "A week or two."

"Tony told me you left the Navy a few years ago. What have you been doing with yourself since then?"

"I work for Sam Dooley. Do you remember him? He was married to my mother for a couple of years."

Sid nodded. "I think I met him once. Seemed like a decent guy."

"He's a good boss. Lets me set my own schedule."

"So what kind of work is it?"

Brock took a long sip of his lemonade, letting the sour liquid wash down the back of his throat. "We help people recover stolen property. Among other things."

"So did you ever marry?" Sid asked. "Kids?"

"I prefer the bachelor life."

Sid sighed. "I was married by the time I was twenty years old. We wanted to have kids right away, but Mother Nature made us wait almost ten years before we had Tony. Then Katie came two years after that." His mouth curved into a wistful smile. "Sure had fun trying, though."

Brock didn't know what to say. How do you reassure a man that his life isn't about to fall apart before his eyes? Living as a bachelor and growing up with a mother who had five divorces under her belt, Brock was hardly qualified to dispense marital advice. So he didn't say anything, just leaned back against the sofa and watched the basketball players run back and forth across the screen.

"Did you see that?" Sid exclaimed, pointing toward the television set. "It was goal-tending."

"How could the ref miss that?" Brock said, watching the replay.

"Rose loves basketball," Sid mused, growing morose once more. "We have season tickets to the Sonics games. I guess I'll let her have them if she wants a divorce."

"I think that's a little premature," Brock said, finishing the last of his lemonade.

"A man's got to be prepared." Sid shook his head. "But I don't know if I'm ready for the single life. The way Kate carries on about it, dating must be hell."

"So tell me about this mystery man of hers," Brock said, his curiosity getting the better of him. "She's convinced he's her Mr. Right."

Sid snorted. "Don't get me started. I think she's crazy to try and snag some man with a skirt."

"Kate told me she and this guy have been e-mailing each other for quite awhile. And he's planning to come to Seattle for a visit soon."

"This isn't one of those Internet romances, is it? The guy could be some kind of psycho stalker."

"I don't think so," Brock said, realizing how little he knew about her so-called "Mr. Perfect." "Kate has good instincts."

"Well, it's hard for me to believe that my Katie is still single after all these years. She's beautiful, bright, independent. Just like her mother. What more could a man want?"

Brock had been asking himself the same question for the past few days. "Maybe it's Kate who is holding back."

Sid nodded. "You're probably right. Too picky. Good thing Rose wasn't that picky or I'd probably still be a bachelor. Do you know where I took her for our first date?"

"Where?"

"My kid brother's Little League game. Hot dogs sold for half price during the seventh inning. I thought that was a real deal." He smiled. "I'm lucky she agreed to go out with me again."

Brock drained his lemonade. "I never asked my mom how she and my dad met. Mom didn't like to talk about him." He set his glass on the coffee table. "Funny, now I kind of wish I knew."

"You can still ask her."

"Maybe I'll do that someday. Not that their love lasted long anyway. Maybe it wasn't love at all." He looked up at Sid. "How the hell is a guy supposed to know when he is in love?"

"Easy," Sid replied. "When you're in love with a woman, the right woman, you can't stop thinking about her. You act like an idiot around her most of the time. And you can't imagine spending the rest of your life with anyone else. Or without her." He stared at the empty flask in his hand, then heaved a long sigh. "Haven't you ever fallen in love, Brock? After all these years?"

He shook his head. "No. I don't think so."

"You'd know," Sid replied, his gaze growing misty and unfocused. "You'd definitely know."

Brock stood up. "I'd better go. It's getting late."

"Stop by again sometime before you leave town." Sid walked with him to the front door. "It's sure been great to see you again."

"I'll do that," Brock promised. "Maybe you can show me what's new in the contracting business."

"You and Tony were the best summer workers I ever had. I wish Tony..." His voice trailed off. "Well, he's happy in Brazil."

"Do you need anything, Sid?" Brock asked, hating to leave the man here all alone. "Groceries or more lemonade mix?"

"No," Sid replied, slapping him on the shoulder. "I'll be just fine. Good night, Brock."

Brock walked to his car, then turned and waited until all the lights in the house went out. It didn't seem right for Sid to be here by himself. Brock remembered how many times he'd sought out the Talaveras' house as a refuge from the cramped, two-bedroom apartment he'd shared with his mother. There was always laughter here—and so much love. He used to dream about having a home like that of his own someday.

When had he decided it was impossible for that dream to come true?

8

KATE TRACKED DOWN Brock in the hotel coffee shop the next morning and wasted no time interrogating him about her father. "Well," she asked, pulling out a chair across from him, "what happened last night?"

"Good morning to you, too," he said, picking up the carafe and pouring her a cup of coffee.

"Sorry," she said, picking up the coffee cup. "I didn't get much sleep last night."

"Your dad is fine," he assured her. "I took him home and we watched a little basketball on television. Talked a little."

"About Mom?"

He nodded. "Sid misses her. I wonder why she really moved out."

Kate cupped her hands around the cup to warm them. "I don't understand it. This is not like my parents. Sure, they fight. Just like any other married couple. But Mom's never actually left before."

"Maybe she really is going through some kind of midlife crisis."

"She's sixty years old," Kate exclaimed. "She should have had her midlife crisis two decades ago."

"People don't live according to schedule," Brock said. "At least, most people."

She knew that was a veiled criticism of her skirt plan, but she let it pass. Convincing Brock that her plan was a sound one wouldn't help her solve this latest crisis. "But why now?"

He shrugged. "It looks to me like Sid and Rose have reached different points in their lives. Your mom is retired and ready to live a little, while your dad is still working a nine-to-five job." A smile tipped up one corner of his mouth. "Or if I know Sid, a nine-to-nine job."

"The business does keep him busy," Kate admitted. "Although it's more by choice than necessity. He always takes on more jobs than he can handle. The least he could do is hire a supervisor or something."

Brock took a bite of his warm cinnamon roll, then washed it down with orange juice. "So have you talked to your mom yet this morning?"

Kate shook her head. "I called my aunt's house a little while ago and Flora said that Mom was out taking her first scuba diving lesson at the Y. Scuba diving! Can you believe it?"

"Sounds like fun."

Kate took a sip of her coffee. "Mom's hobbies used to be ceramics and macramé."

Brock smiled. "Maybe she just wanted to try something new and daring."

"That's what I'm afraid of," Kate admitted softly. "Maybe she wants a new life and a new place to live to go along with her new hobby."

"I guess this puts a big hitch in your anniversary party plans."

She tipped up her chin. "I'm not canceling the party. This separation is only temporary. It has to be."

"Are you sure you want to take that chance? There are a lot of people coming to celebrate. Or maybe you should tell Sid and Rose about it. I'm sure they'd agree to set aside their differences for one night and put on a good show for everybody."

"That's exactly what I don't want." Kate leaned forward. "I want it to be real. My parents have been married forty years. *Forty years!* That's longer than either you or I have been alive. It's supposed to be something to celebrate, not fake your way through."

Brock took the last bite of his roll, then sucked a smudge of gooey icing off his thumb. "So what's your solution?"

"We have to find a way to get them back together."

He arched a brow. "We?"

"Will you help me?" she entreated, knowing she was asking a lot of him. "Dad likes you so much,

Brock. I think he'll listen to you. And I'll work on Mom."

He looked doubtful. "The party is just over a week away."

"We have to try."

Brock stared at her long enough to make Kate squirm in her chair. Just yesterday she'd told herself to keep her distance from him and now she was recruiting him to help reunite her parents.

"Sid really is lost without Rose," Brock said at last. "That much was clear last night."

Relief flowed through her. "So you'll help me?"

He looked into her eyes. "I'll do anything to make you happy, Kate."

She leaned back in her chair, a little flustered by his words. "Thank you, Brock. You don't know how much this means to me."

He pushed his empty plate away. "What exactly do you want me to do?"

She shrugged. "I don't know exactly. Maybe you can give Dad some suggestions on ways to win Mom back. Bring some romance into their marriage again."

"Me?" he asked, a half smile curving his mouth "What makes you think I have expertise in that area?"

She rolled her eyes. "Come on, Brock. Tony told

me about your infamous Navy days. Didn't you have a girl in every port?"

His smile widened into a wolfish grin. "Well, not every port. Greenland was a little scarce of women. Although I do remember a blonde..."

"Spare me the details," she muttered, a twinge of jealousy pricking her, even though she knew he was just teasing. Or maybe not. Kate had no doubt that Brock Gannon could have any woman he wanted.

"Okay," he said, standing up. "Operation Talavera begins today. I'll invite your dad to a sports bar for supper tonight. There's a great game between the Lakers and the Knicks."

"And I'll try to catch Mom between scuba diving lessons," Kate said wryly.

"In the meantime, we have a date with a mugger." Brock stood up. "Are you ready to go?"

She smiled and rose to her feet. "I guess there are worse hobbies than scuba diving."

Twenty minutes later, they pulled up to an apartment complex just off Stewart Street. "You stay here," Brock said, opening the driver's door of the Camaro. "I'll be right back."

"I'm coming with you," Kate replied, climbing out of the car and following him to the front door. "She's an old lady. She might be intimidated if she sees a big, strange man standing outside her door."

"This old lady nailed that cabbie with her purse

and made off with half the stuff in his cab. I'm the one who should be intimidated."

"Then I'll come along to protect you," she quipped, as she preceded him into the building.

They climbed the three flights of stairs that led to Petula Clarkson's apartment. The door stood half open, barely hanging on its hinges. No light came from inside.

Brock took one step across the threshold. "Ms. Clarkson? Are you in here?"

Silence. Brock walked in a few more steps, then returned to the hallway. "It's deserted and the place is a mess. Looks like we missed a good brawl."

Kate groaned. "So where is Petula Clarkson?"

A voice sounded behind them. "Try the city jail. The cops came late last night and took all of them away."

Brock and Kate both turned to see a young teenage girl lounging in the door frame across from the Clarkson apartment. She had on a white T-shirt, the neck stretched out far enough to reveal a heart tattoo near her collarbone. Her dishwater blond hair hung uncombed around her thin shoulders. A cigarette dangled from the fingers of her right hand.

"What happened?" Brock asked.

"I called them," the girl replied. "You should of heard all the racket. I thought those two guys were going to kill each other over that stuck-up witch."

"They were fighting over Petula Clarkson?" Kate asked.

The kid snorted. "No, not her. I'm talking about her granddaughter, Desiree. She comes out into the hallway, flouncing her stuff around in that flimsy blouse and shiny new black skirt. Suddenly, Rocky and Bud, who have been best buddies since grade school and can't stand snooty Desi, start going nuts over her. Next thing I know, they're rolling on the floor, throwing punches."

"So she had on a new black skirt?" Kate said, giving Brock an I-told-you-so glance.

"That's right. Said her grandma gave it to her for her birthday."

"How well do you know the Clarksons?" Brock asked.

The girl took a long drag of her cigarette, then blew a perfect smoke ring in the air. "Long enough to know this isn't the old lady's first trip to the slammer. She steals stuff to support her bingo habit. Even took our Christmas wreath off the front door one year and sold it down at Charlie's Consignment Shop."

"Did Desiree go to jail, too?" Kate asked.

The girl shook her head. "No, although she deserved to, since she's the one who started all of it. The cops gave her a ride downtown to file a report. I don't know where she is now."

"Was she still wearing the skirt last night?"

"Yeah. And those two cops were really giving her the eye, if you know what I mean. *Sheesh*. Men."

"Thanks," Kate said, as she and Brock headed for the stairs.

"Sounds like your magic skirt is wreaking havoc." Brock held the door of the apartment building open for her.

"Now do you believe me?"

He shook his head. "Men have been fighting over women since the beginning of time. I doubt the skirt had anything to do with it."

Their next stop was the police station.

"Yes, we do have a Petula Clarkson in custody." The officer at the front desk pushed his glasses up on his nose. "She's charged with assault and theft. She had a bail hearing this afternoon but couldn't come up with enough money. Are you her family or her lawyers?"

"Neither," Brock said. "But we'd like to speak with her."

"I'll see what I can do."

Thirty minutes later, they were escorted into a holding cell. A plump, white-haired woman with apple cheeks and bright blue eyes sat on a wooden bench.

"Ms. Clarkson?" Kate ventured.

The older woman's eyes narrowed. "Who wants to know?"

"I'm Kate Tal..." Kate looked up at Brock, then down at his hand squeezing her arm.

"We're here to get information," he admonished under his breath. "Not give it. Especially to a thief."

She nodded, then started over. "We're here about the skirt you took from the taxi yesterday afternoon. It was black, hanging in a drycleaner's bag."

Petula Clarkson sniffed. "There's no proof I took it or anything else from that cab." She heaved a pitiful sigh. "I'm just a frail, sick, old woman. You can't imagine what this cold, damp place is doing to my arthritis."

Kate actually found the room rather comfortable— not that she'd want to spend any length of time here. But it certainly wasn't quite as horrible as Petula painted it.

"All we care about is the skirt," Brock persisted. "And we're willing to put up your bail money to get it."

"Brock," Kate hissed under her breath, furious with him for not consulting with her about this. It was one thing to bribe a waiter or two for information, quite another to let a criminal back out onto the streets. Of course, this particular criminal didn't look all that dangerous. Still, Kate had seen the nasty lump on the back of the cabbie's head.

He ignored her entreaty. "That's the offer. Take it or leave it."

Petula pursed her lips. "Well, now that I think about it, there was a black skirt in the box of items I told my granddaughter to take to Charlie's."

"The consignment store?" Kate asked.

The old woman nodded. "That's right. Desiree wanted to keep it, but I need to raise money for bail. So she promised to take it to the store. A nice skirt like that should fetch a pretty price." Her expression turned shrewd. "Wish I'd have known how much you two wanted it. I would have kept it and sold it to you myself."

Kate could just imagine the price the woman would charge. She already owed Brock too much money. And now Petula's bail would be added to the tab.

"What's the address of the consignment store?" Brock asked.

"It's near the Pike Place Market," Petula replied. "On Stewart Street. And don't forget to pay my bail before you leave."

The guard unlocked the cell and escorted Brock and Kate back to the front desk.

"Are we really going to pay her bail?"

He turned to her. "You can't make bargains if you don't intend to keep them."

"But she could be lying about the skirt."

"That's why we're going to check out the consignment store before we shell out one dime."

9

"THIS PLACE IS GREAT!"

Brock looked up from the rack of skirts in front of him to see Kate admiring all the vintage knickknacks on the shelves of the consignment store.

"We're here to look for the skirt, remember?"

"I know, but how can you resist this stuff?" She picked up a pair of colored glass balls, each attached to a string and connected with a plastic ring at the top. "Look at these. What were they called?"

"Clackers," he said, remembering how he'd had more than one set confiscated for playing with them at school. "I don't think they make them anymore."

She tried to swing the balls upward to clack them together and ended up whacking herself on the cheek with them. "I can see why."

"Ooh, look at this!" She put down the Clackers and moved onto the next item. "A mood ring. I wonder if it still works."

Her delight in finding these old fad treasures made him smile. It all looked like junk to him. "Why don't you try it on and see."

She slipped the mood ring onto her index finger, then waited for the stone to turn color. "It's blue...no green." She looked up at him, her eyes sparkling. "I wish I could remember what mood that color stands for."

He sucked in his breath, suddenly feeling a whole new mood descending on him. The way Kate looked at him made his body heat like a flash fire. He wanted her so damn bad that he couldn't even try to deny it to himself anymore. Maybe she was right. Maybe the skirt was making him crazy. He'd certainly never felt like this with any woman before.

Then again, he'd never known another woman as special as Kate.

She reached out and grabbed his arm, the mood ring forgotten. "I don't believe it."

He followed her gaze. "What? Do you see the skirt?"

"No. A Lava lamp."

"A Lava lamp?" He echoed, wondering what she found so fascinating about it.

"They were the big fad in the sixties. My parents got married in 1965. Wouldn't Lava lamps make a great centerpiece for the tables at the party?"

"Exactly how many Lava lamps would you need?"

"With ten guests per table and a total of two hundred guests coming to the party..." She paused, doing the calculation in her head. "I'd say about twenty lamps would do it."

His gaze scanned the shelf. "Too bad. There are only five here."

"But the city is full of thrift shops. I'm sure you could find more."

He had promised to help her with the party. And the way she was looking at him made it impossible to refuse her anything. To think about anything but touching her again. Feeling the softness of her skin beneath his hands. He wanted to taste her. To feel her moving against him.

"Brock?"

His eyes flew open, his body rock hard and his breathing uneven. "What?"

"You're so quiet. Are you tired?"

"No," he said, although that was a lie. He was tired of fighting his feelings for her. Tired of just imagining himself holding Kate. Kissing her all over. Making love to her.

She fingered the polyester clothes on the rack in front of her. "I just had a great idea."

He desperately hoped it involved getting naked together. "I'm open for anything."

She turned to him, a wide smile on her face. "What if we give the party a 'Return to the Sixties' theme? We could hand out love beads and headbands at the door. Have the D.J. play music from the sixties. People could even wear vintage clothes if they wanted. Most of the guests sent their RSVP by e-mail, so I could send a blanket e-mail and give them the option. It could be a lot of fun."

"I thought you wanted to wear the skirt for the party." His jaw tightened. "For Mr. Perfect."

"Actually, Mr. Perfect and I are going out before the party." She turned to the rack of clothing and began sorting through it.

His body tensed. "When?"

She shrugged. "As soon as he arrives in Seattle. His plans aren't set yet. I'm sure he'll be e-mailing me when they are."

Brock felt as if he'd been hit by a freight train. "Great."

She nodded. "Now you know why I'm so anxious to find the skirt. Time is running out."

Brock walked to another clothes rack, giving himself time to think. She was right about one thing. Time was running out. His plan was to secure the skirt and immediately transport it to Calabra. But what if he didn't get his hands on the skirt before the party? What reason could he give for sticking around Seattle until he found it?

Or worse, what if he found it before the party...? He looked up to see Kate talking to one of the young male clerks at the cash register. Finding the skirt for her date with this Mr. Perfect meant so much to her.

What would it hurt for him to let her wear it before he took it and left Seattle? Not that he believed the skirt was anything more than a scrap of fabric. But she believed it. And at this moment, making her happy seemed like the most important mission he'd ever been on.

Even if the thought of Kate in another man's arms made him feel like hell.

Kate walked back over to the clothes rack. "They sold the skirt already. Wally, the guy who works here, said one of their regular customers snatched it up as soon as it came in the store."

"Did you get a name?"

"Carla Corona," she replied with a proud smile. "And it only cost me five dollars. I guess people in Seattle have a lower bribe rate than some of the other places you've worked."

Brock had a feeling the clerk's eagerness to help had more to do with her incredible body than her pocketbook. But he wasn't about to tell her that. "So where do we go from here?"

She glanced at her watch. "I hate to say it, but I have to go back to work. It's getting close to noon and I'd like to swing by a grocery store first, if you don't mind. I want to pick up a few items for me and some frozen dinners for Dad. Despite what he says, I know he's not eating right. Could you drop them off at the house for me later?"

"Sure. And I'll spend this afternoon seeing what information I can dig up on this Carla Corona."

"Okay, as long as you keep me posted."

They made a quick trip to the grocery store, then returned to the Hartington. Brock helped her carry the grocery sacks to her room.

"I've got exactly two minutes to get down to that conference luncheon," Kate said, hastily shoving her plastic key card into the lock. She pushed the door open. "Do you mind separating out the frozen dinners for Dad and sticking them in the freezer? I'll put the rest away later."

"No problem," Brock said, following her into the room.

Kate stopped short in front of him and his momentum almost knocked her over. "Look."

"What's wrong?" But his nose told him before she could. There were flowers everywhere. Bountiful bouquets of roses, orchids and lilies. The room smelled like someone had spilled an industrial bottle of perfume.

"I don't believe this." Dropping the grocery sacks onto the table, Kate reached for the small envelope nestled in the bouquet of red roses nearest to her. She smiled when she read the card.

"Well?" he asked, still holding a sack in each arm. "Who's your admirer?"

"It's...him," she replied, tucking the card back in

the envelope and setting it on the table. "Mr. Perfect. He's here."

A lead weight settled in the pit of his stomach. "In Seattle? Already?"

She nodded, a pink blush suffusing her cheeks. "He just arrived this morning. The card said he wanted it to be a surprise."

"I hate surprises." Brock looked at the clock. "It's two minutes after twelve."

"The luncheon!" She hurried to the door. "I've got to go. Let me know what you find out about the Corona woman. And say hello to my dad for me."

She was out the door before he could reply. Brock set down the groceries, then picked up the envelope she had opened only minutes before. He knew it would be an invasion of her privacy to read it, but he'd already broken into her family home and her hotel room. So he wasn't about to let a pang of guilt or two stop him now.

His gaze scanned the card, then dropped to the signature on the bottom. The name left him cold. Todd Winslow. He let the card drop to the table.

Kate thought her Mr. Perfect was Todd *Scumbag* Winslow? That wasn't his legal middle name, of course. It was the one Brock had given him right before he'd dropped the jerk with a solid right hook twelve years ago. And in his opinion, it certainly fit Winslow better than Mr. Perfect.

It was one thing to imagine Kate trying to seduce some faceless, nameless stranger with this skirt. But now that he knew Todd Winslow was the intended prey in her marriage trap, he had even more incentive than ever to get his hands on that skirt before she did. Winslow had been an arrogant punk in high school and Brock didn't have any reason to believe he had changed.

The only question was why had this jerk developed a sudden interest in Kate? Did Winslow just want the thrill of a one-night stand with his old next-door neighbor while he was in Seattle? Or was there something more to it?

Brock paced back and forth across the small living-room area, his fists clenched. But what the hell could he do? The aroma from the flowers was making him sick to his stomach. Or maybe it was the thought of Winslow holding Kate. Kissing her. Making love to her.

"Not in a million years," he muttered, pulling all the frozen dinners out of the sacks and sticking them in the freezer compartment of the suite's refrigerator. Then he slammed the freezer door shut. No way would he let her wear the skirt now. Not for Winslow.

Which meant it was time to come up with a new plan.

IT WAS EARLY evening by the time Kate got back to her hotel room. The heavy aroma of the hothouse flowers greeted her when she opened the door, lifting her spirits. It had been a chaotic day at work, with Murphy's Law working overtime. The only bright spot had been a telephone call from Todd. He was staying with his parents and wanted to take her out for dinner tonight. But she'd declined, making up some excuse about working late.

She couldn't meet him without wearing the skirt, even if she didn't look like the same tubby teenager he probably remembered. She wanted to make a new first impression that would last a lifetime. Kicking off her shoes, she walked over to the kitchenette. Brock had put all her groceries away and there weren't any frozen dinners in the freezer compartment, which meant he must have already left for the house.

A knock on the door made her turn. Her first thought was that it was Todd. She reached up to straighten her hair, then looked down at the jade green pantsuit she was wearing, chosen for comfort rather than style. Kate thought about not answering the door, but the knock came again, louder this time.

"This is ridiculous," she muttered, moving toward the door. She wasn't going to hide from him. Even without the skirt, she wasn't exactly the hunchback of Notre Dame. Opening the door, she was surprised to find her mother standing on the other side.

"Mom!"

"Hi, sweetie." Rose walked into the room wearing a dress that Kate had never seen before. "Flora told me you called a couple of times today looking for me."

"A couple of times?" Kate closed the door, then turned and planted her hands on her hips. "Try ten. Where have you been all day?"

"Well, after my scuba diving lessons, I drove out to Old Baldy Mountain. Haven't been there in ages. Your father and I took a weekend trip out there when you and Tony were just babies. There's a beautiful inn near there now. I'd love to go back and stay sometime."

"Maybe you and Dad could go there for a second honeymoon."

Rose's mouth thinned. "I assume your father has told you the news?"

"Last night." Kate dropped down into the armchair. "Mom, how could this happen?"

"We've grown apart," Rose replied. "And I don't want to spend my golden years waiting for your father to come home from work."

"But did you have to leave? Isn't that a little drastic? Couldn't you have gone to marriage counseling together or something?"

"You know your father," Rose said. "He won't

even admit there is a problem, much less pay a marriage counselor to solve it."

"But you'd be willing to go to a counselor if he agreed?" Kate persisted.

Rose shrugged her shoulders. "Maybe. As long as it didn't interfere with my schedule."

Kate frowned. "What schedule?"

"I have scuba diving lessons every Monday, Wednesday and Friday. And I just joined a bridge club that meets on Tuesdays and Thursdays."

"But you don't know how to play bridge."

"Then it's about time I learned. Besides, this club is for people at all levels. It's not like that cut-throat group of women your Aunt Flora plays with."

"Anything else?" Kate asked, wondering how long her mother had wanted to play bridge and scuba dive.

Rose smiled. "I'm thinking of taking a Chinese cooking class."

"Dad hates Chinese food."

"I love it," her mother countered. "I'm through living my life just to please him. It's time I start thinking about my own happiness for a change."

Kate swallowed. She had only a few short days to bring her parents back together. At this moment, she wasn't sure she could accomplish it even if she had a century to do it. Rose seemed both resigned and resolute.

"Don't you love Dad anymore?" Kate asked softly.

Rose reached out to gently squeeze her hand. "Of course I love him. I love him with all my heart. But I never see him. When I was teaching, I was too busy to notice how much time we spent apart. But since I've retired, I've come to realize how little we see each other. I get up in the morning to make his lunch, then he goes off to work while I sit home and wait. And wait and wait and wait. I'm tired of waiting, Katie. I'm ready to live my life."

"But can't you take scuba lessons and play bridge and learn to cook Chinese food without moving out of the house. Without leaving Dad?"

"It's more than that," Rose said. "I want to go to new places and see things I've only heard about. I want to spend some of the money your father and I have worked and scraped so hard to save for all of these years. But I don't want to do it alone."

How could Kate argue with that? "I know Dad really misses you."

Rose's mouth curved into a wistful smile. "I miss him, too. I'm not sleeping too well without him snoring beside me. Guess I've grown used to it over the years."

"Is there anything I can do?" Kate asked, not ready to give up.

"Just promise me you won't worry." Then Rose

looked around the room, as if noticing the flowers for the first time. "What's all this?"

Kate smiled. "They're from...a friend."

Rose arched a brow. "Looks like he's more than a friend to me."

"They're from the man I was telling you about before. The one I think might be perfect for me." Kate wondered why she was so reluctant to tell her mother the man was Todd, especially after the way Rose had raved about him. But she didn't have the time to analyze it now.

Rose got up and walked over to the bouquet of champagne roses on the television set. She inhaled deeply. "They're beautiful, Katie. Just beautiful."

"He asked me out for dinner tonight," Kate confided.

"And here I am taking up time you need to get ready for your date!"

Kate shook her head. "No, I'm not going. I told him I had to work."

Rose cocked her head to one side. "You don't look very busy to me. Are you playing hard to get?"

Kate laughed. "I'm almost twenty-eight years old, Mom. I can't afford to play hard to get anymore. But I can't see him until I'm wearing the skirt."

"So what's the problem?"

"It's disappeared. I left it in a taxi and...well, it's a long story. But Brock's helping me look for it." Too late she remembered that her mother didn't know yet that Brock was back in town.

Rose's eyes widened. "Brock? You don't mean Brock Gannon?"

She nodded. "One and the same."

"What's he doing back in Seattle?"

"I'm not sure," Kate hedged. "He's staying here at the hotel and we've run into each other a time or two."

"I don't believe it," Rose exclaimed, shaking her head in wonder. "Why, I haven't set eyes on that boy since he was a teenager. How is he?"

She smiled. "I think the word incredible would describe him accurately."

Rose laughed. "I knew he'd turn into a real lady-killer, despite those bumpy years he had growing up. It's those eyes."

"And the face and the body and that deep voice that makes you feel all shivery inside."

"You sure you want to wear the skirt for this other guy?" Rose asked, her keen perception making Kate a bit uncomfortable. "It sounds like Brock has certainly captured your attention. Of course, there's nothing wrong with having two men interested in you. That's a situation any woman would envy."

"Brock isn't interested in me," Kate replied. "Well, I mean he is, but..."

"But what?"

"But he saw me in the skirt and had the same reaction that Gwen and Chelsea both described."

"So you don't think his interest is sincere?"

Kate nibbled her lip. "I'm not sure what to think." Then she realized they were talking about her love life instead of saving her parents' marriage. "Will you at least call Dad? Try to talk things out?"

Rose hesitated, then shook her head. "I'm going to wait for him to call me. As far as I know, he doesn't even miss me!"

"Yes he does, Mother. You should have heard him last night. He's like a lost soul."

"I know you think I'm being hard on your father, Katie, but I've been married to the man for almost forty years and I don't feel like I really know him anymore." She sighed. "I wish there was some way we could fall in love all over again."

Kate's heart skittered at the despair she heard in her mother's voice. "Just please promise me you won't give up too soon."

"I promise." Rose stood up and walked to the door, turning as she opened it. "We Talavera women never give up. You remember that."

Kate walked over and kissed her mother's powdered cheek. "I will."

When she was alone once more, Kate let her gaze drift over the assortment of bouquets adorning the room. They truly were beautiful. Todd was not only successful, but thoughtful as well. And obviously interested in pursuing a relationship with her. So why was she suddenly having second thoughts?

Her mother was right. Talavera women never gave up. It was time to find the skirt.

10

A COUPLE OF DAYS LATER, Kate drove her Dodge Intrepid along Jackson Street. "Are you sure we should just show up unannounced? How do we know this Carla Corona will even let us inside?"

Brock sat in the passenger seat beside her. "We'll have the element of surprise on our side. And haven't you ever heard the expression, money talks?"

"Maybe for some people," Kate admitted. "Okay, most people. But you can't buy everyone, Brock. Sometimes there are things more important than money."

He didn't say anything for a long moment. "If Carla is shopping at consignment stores, then money is obviously important to her."

"So tell me about her. What did you find out? She's not another felon like Petula, is she?"

He shook his head. "Not according to my information. Carla Corona is a law-abiding beautician. Twenty-four years old. Married. Blond hair and green eyes. Five foot four, weighs about one hundred and thirty pounds, and wears contact lenses."

"Is that all?" Kate asked, amazed at his resources.

"She's allergic to cats," he quipped, "but I don't think that will affect our mission."

"Mission," she echoed with a laugh. "I feel like some superspy. Although I doubt anyone has ever been after a skirt before."

He turned his attention to the window. "Any more flowers from Winslow?"

She glanced at him. "You looked at the card."

"It was right in front of me. I couldn't resist." He turned back to her. "Besides, snooping around is part of my job. It's what I do best. It's the reason we found Petula. And Carla."

"Do you like your work, Brock?" Kate asked suddenly.

"What do you mean?"

"I mean, the things you have to do get information. Bribing waiters and old ladies. Snooping around for clues. Does it ever bother you?"

He considered her question for a moment. "I guess I've gotten used to it. I like setting my own hours and doing the job my way. I found out in the Navy that I'm not very good at taking orders."

She nodded. "That's the reason my dad says he likes working as a contractor. He's the one in charge, although he still has to do the work he's been hired to do."

"Tony and I used to talk about going to work for your dad," Brock told her. "Or starting up a contracting business of our own."

She pulled up to a red light. "So why didn't you?"

He shrugged. "My plans changed after I got kicked out of school. I decided the Navy was my best option. So I enlisted, earned my GED, and never looked back."

"I never found out what the fight was about. Or why you started it."

"And you never told me if Winslow sent you any more flowers. Trying to change the subject?"

"No, but it sounds like that's what you're trying to do."

"You're very perceptive, Kate." The tone of his voice made her glance at him. He'd been acting a little odd today. As if he had something else on his mind.

She thought about pushing him to answer her question, but realized he still might be sensitive about it. Her instincts told her Brock Gannon was a very proud man. So she decided to answer his question instead. "Todd hasn't sent me any more flowers, but he has phoned a couple of times. He's staying at his parents' house."

Brock nodded. "So that explains the black Lexus sedan parked at the Winslows'."

"I really don't want to see him until I'm wearing the skirt, but I'm starting to run out of good excuses." She rounded the street corner and pulled up to a ranch-style house with powder pink siding and white shutters. "If I'm lucky, we'll leave here today with the skirt and I won't need any excuses anymore."

Brock climbed slowly out of the car. He suddenly hoped Carla Corona wasn't at home. That fate had miraculously stepped in to prevent the inevitable.

But the door opened before Kate even rang the doorbell. A young woman looked curiously at them. "Yes? Can I help you?"

"Carla Corona?" Kate asked.

The woman hesitated. "Yes. Who are you?"

"I'm Kate and this is Brock," she said, sliding a glance in his direction.

He knew she didn't like his rule of holding back their last names. It still amazed him how trusting she was. And gave him even more reason to want to protect her from someone like Winslow. He had to keep telling himself that or he'd never be able to go through with this.

"We want to talk to you about the black skirt you purchased at Charlie's Consignment Shop a couple of days ago," Kate continued. "I'm very interested in buying it from you."

"Wally sent you?" Carla asked, her wariness fading a little.

Kate smiled. "If Wally is a skinny kid with red hair and glasses, then yes, he's the one who gave us your name. I hope you don't mind our just stopping by like this."

"I guess not." She held the door open wider. "Please come on in."

Brock followed Kate into the small living room. Carla's home was decorated with all kinds of vintage pieces. Brock shrugged out of his jacket and laid it on the arm of a fingerback sofa, then sat down next to Kate.

Carla took a seat in an antique rocker. "Charlie's is one of my favorite consignment stores. As you can see, I'm something of a collector, although the skirt wasn't vintage. I just couldn't resist it. I've never seen fabric quite like that before."

"It is unusual," Kate agreed. "I accidentally left the skirt in a taxi, and it eventually found its way to the consignment shop. I'm very anxious to get it back and am willing to reimburse you the thirty dollars you paid for it."

Carla hesitated.

"Fifty dollars," Kate offered, a note of desperation in her voice.

Brock forced himself to contribute to the conversation. "We'll go as high as one hundred. The skirt has a lot of sentimental value for us."

Carla shook her head. "I'm sorry, but even if I wanted to sell it to you, I couldn't."

Kate's face fell. "Why not?"

"Because it's gone."

"Gone?" Brock and Kate echoed together.

"My husband and I took the ferry to Victoria yesterday. I wore the skirt." Carla cleared her throat. "We eventually found ourselves on the starboard side of the deck, behind a big tarp...completely out of sight of the other passengers. One thing led to another, and the next thing I knew the skirt was flying overboard, along with my husband's tie and jacket."

Kate swallowed hard. "Overboard? You mean, in Puget Sound?"

Carla nodded, a pink blush suffusing her cheeks. "My husband got a little carried away. If you want to know the truth, I've never seen him like that before. He's usually so staid and sedate." Her face took on a warm glow. "It was wonderful."

"The skirt...sunk?" Kate asked, as if still not quite able to absorb this latest turn of events.

The woman shrugged her thin shoulders. "I suppose it might have floated for a little while. Or got caught in the boat's propeller and ripped to pieces." Her blush deepened. "I had to stay hidden behind the tarp until my husband bought a towel from the *Victoria Clipper's* gift shop for me to wear around my waist. It was so embarrassing."

Kate sank back against the sofa. Gone. The skirt was gone. After all her planning. All her dreams for the future. It was over.

"I'm so sorry," Carla said, wringing her hands together. "I had no idea the skirt belonged to you or that you were looking for it."

"It's all right," Kate replied, her voice hollow.

Brock reached out and squeezed her hand, threading his broad fingers through her own. "You okay?"

She nodded, then rose to her feet. "I'm fine. But I think we'd better go. We've taken up enough of Mrs. Corona's time."

"I have a couple of black skirts in my closet," Carla offered. "They're not as nice as the other one, but if you're desperate..."

"Thanks, but I'll work something out," Kate replied, giving her a wobbly smile before she quickly headed out the door.

"Are you sure you're all right?" Brock asked, as he followed her to the car.

"I don't get it, Brock," she said, walking briskly and looking straight ahead. "Why is fate so determined that I stay single? Every time I get close to finding the right guy, *Bam!* fate steps in and snatches him away." She stopped at the curb and turned to face him. "What am I doing wrong? All I want is a man who will love me. Marriage and a family. Is that so much to ask?"

He swallowed hard, his throat tight. "I think you're asking the wrong guy, Kate. I don't believe in fate. I think sometimes life just knocks people around for the fun of it. We have to find a way to survive. Happiness is a fringe benefit for those lucky enough to find it." He reached his hand out to touch her, then pulled back. "But if anyone deserves to be happy, you do, Kate."

She took a deep, shuddering breath. "Thanks, Brock. And I'm sorry for whining. I'll be fine. I just have to get used to the idea that the skirt is gone."

He gave her a brisk nod. "I forgot my jacket. Wait here, I'll be right back."

"Take your time, Brock. I need to check my messages anyway."

He watched Kate climb into the car and pull her cell phone out of her purse. Then he headed back toward the house.

Carla stood just inside the front door with his jacket in her hands. She handed it to Brock. "Here you go."

"Thanks," he muttered, folding the coat over his arm.

"No, thank you," Carla replied with a grin. "I've never made five hundred dollars quite so easily before. The skirt is tucked in the sleeve of your jacket, just like you instructed."

"Good," he said, feeling like a worm. He'd had no idea that Kate would take the loss of the skirt so hard. Was her heart really that set on winning Winslow?

Carla held up the wad of one hundred dollar bills she'd pulled out of his coat pocket. "I guess those drama classes I took in high school came in handy after all."

He turned without a word and headed toward Kate's car. Making the deal with Carla Corona ahead of time was one of the lowest things he'd ever done. But what choice did he have? His mission was to recover the skirt and he'd accomplished it. Besides, would he rather that Kate wore the skirt for Winslow? If she did, the next Talavera party would probably be her wedding reception.

He shook his head, disgusted with himself. He didn't really believe the skirt had any special powers, did he? Despite Kate's adamant claims to the contrary, he didn't. No. Of course not.

But he wasn't about to take any chances when Kate's happiness was at stake.

Then he opened the car door and found her crying her eyes out.

Brock slid into the passenger seat and pulled her into his arms. "Kate, what's wrong?"

"Nothing," she said with a hiccup. "I'm fine. Really. Just ignore me."

But that was impossible when he could feel her hot tears seeping through the fabric of his shirt. "Kate, what is it? Are you that upset about the skirt?"

She swallowed back her tears, then gave him a shaky smile. "I guess it's a combination of losing the skirt, the stress of planning the party and Mom and Dad's separation. But mostly it's because of Tony's wonderful news. He just left me a message on my answering machine."

"What wonderful news?"

"His wife Elena is pregnant."

He reached up and ran his fingers through her silky hair. His heart contracted at the sight of her tear-streaked face. "Congratulations, Aunt Kate."

"Thank you." She wiped the tears from her cheeks. "According to Tony's message they're both flying in the day of the party. They're going to wait until then to tell Mom and Dad. Of course, Tony doesn't know about the separation yet. I didn't want him to worry."

Brock wiped away a stray tear off her cheek with his thumb. "That seems to run in your family. Are you sure you're okay?"

She nodded, but her mouth trembled a little. "I'm sorry. I don't know what came over me. I never cry."

"It's all right," he breathed, then leaned forward

and kissed one tear-streaked cheek, tasting the saltiness on his lips. He gently kissed the other cheek as her thick eyelashes fanned against his brow. He kissed the corner of her mouth, then let his lips brush along the length of her jaw.

"Brock, I..."

But he stopped her words with his mouth, savoring the sweet taste of her. How could Kate ever believe she needed some silly skirt to make a man fall for her? She certainly deserved someone better than Winslow.

And she deserved someone better than Brock.

What did he have to offer her? He was a high school dropout with nothing more than a GED and a stint in the Navy on his résumé. He could hardly include his mercenary experience, since his missions had led him into more than one shady dealing. Like the one he'd just made with Carla Corona. Maybe not illegal, but certainly not honorable either. He'd grown up learning how to fend for himself—and it had made him a wealthy man.

But he knew Kate wouldn't be impressed with money. He wanted her to be proud of him, but past experience had taught him that he'd always come up short. Hell, his own father had never wanted him. And Kate wouldn't want him either—not if she learned about his deal with Carla.

He abruptly pulled away from her, disgusted with

himself all over again. "We'd better go. I'm supposed to meet your dad at one of his job sites this afternoon."

She stared at him for a moment, then turned toward the dashboard and flipped on the ignition. He could see her hands shaking slightly as she gripped the steering wheel.

"Thank you, Brock," she said, pulling into the lane of traffic.

Her gratitude made him wince. "For what?"

"For helping me search for the skirt. I really do appreciate all your help, even if we weren't successful. And I definitely intend to reimburse you for all your expenses."

He shifted in his seat, feeling the soft lump of the skirt in the jacket he held on his lap. Now he felt even lower than a worm. He felt like worm excrement. "Forget about it."

"No," she said, shaking her head. "I can't just forget it. Not after everything you've done."

He leaned his head against the door window and closed his eyes, a headache throbbing against his temple and her words echoing in his brain. *Everything he'd done.*

If she only knew.

11

KATE COULDN'T GET away from Brock fast enough. She made some lame excuse about a last-minute meeting, then escaped to her hotel suite via the employee service elevator.

She was mortified at breaking down in front of him. Her cheeks burned, as much from the memory of his kisses as her tears. Dropping onto the sofa, she buried her face in her hands. Why had he kissed her? Was it out of concern? Pity? That thought made her feel slightly sick. She didn't want Brock's sympathy. Or have him believe she was so desperate that she needed a skirt to attract a man.

Which brought up an even bigger question. Why had he stopped kissing her and pulled away like that? Was he afraid of giving her the wrong idea? He'd made no secret of the fact that he wasn't sticking around Seattle for long. Perhaps he thought he was being noble, afraid of leading her on.

She shook her head, more confused than ever. Brock wanted her, she'd known that since the day he saw her wearing the skirt. But his kisses today hadn't been driven by lust. They'd been sweet. Tender. And so loving a lump rose in her throat at the thought of being cherished like that by a man. But for every day of her life, not just a few stolen moments in a car.

The telephone rang, giving her a much needed break from her impending pity party. She picked up the receiver and cleared her voice, secretly hoping it was Brock. "Hello?"

"This time, I'm not taking no for an answer."

She smiled. "Hi, Todd."

"Dinner at Canlis. Eight o'clock. I'll be the guy nervously pacing in the foyer, worried that you won't show up."

She laughed, wondering why she'd been so reticent to meet him. It was just Todd, the boy she'd known since she was five years old. "Okay."

"Okay? Is that a yes? Can I have that in writing, Ms. Talavera?"

Time to stop stalling. She was determined to put Brock Gannon out of her mind once and for all. "I'll be there. I promise."

"Great. Fantastic." He lowered his voice a notch. "I can't wait to see you again, Kate."

She hung up the phone, already mentally sorting through her closet for something to wear. All these weeks, she'd planned on wearing the skirt, certain it would do all the work for her. Now she'd have to impress Todd all on her own. At least, this way, if it worked out between them, she'd never have to wonder if he really wanted her or had been seduced by the skirt.

Squaring her shoulders, she marched into her bedroom and dug through the closet, finally pulling out a dress she'd bought in New York on a dare from Chelsea. The red strapless cocktail dress had a few magical effects of its own. The cut of the gown enhanced her cleavage and narrowed her waist and the abbreviated hemline showed off her legs to her best advantage.

After laying the gown on her bed, she reapplied her makeup, then swept her hair up into a French roll. For once, her unruly curls cooperated, but she gave them a good spritz with hairspray just to avoid any last-minute rebellions. She found the perfect shade of lipstick to match the dress in her makeup bag and a brand-new pair of nylons in her dresser.

Maybe fate was on her side after all.

Slipping into a pair of red heels that had cost her more than a day's pay, she took one last look in the mirror, then transferred her car keys, lipstick and billfold into an evening bag and headed for the door. Kate was surprised at how calm she was about her impending date with Todd. She'd been dreaming about this meeting ever since he'd replied to the party invitation. Now the time had finally come.

And she intended to make the most of it.

THE DOORS of the elevator opened on the third floor of the hotel and Brock blinked at the vision in front of him. "Kate? Is that you?"

"Hello, Brock. I was just on my way out."

His gaze moved from elegant twist in her hair, all the way down to her feet, and back again. His brain-waves momentarily malfunctioned and he was unable to speak. Then he took a deep breath and tried to pretend she wasn't the most stunning woman he'd ever seen. "Your dad and I are going to bowl a few games at Roxbury Lanes. I came up to see if you'd like to come along."

She stepped into the elevator with him and pushed the button for the first floor. "Thanks, Brock. Any other time, I'd love to, but I already have plans tonight."

The elevator doors closed and his heart lurched. "With Todd?"

She nodded. "He just called. We're going out for dinner."

He folded his arms across his chest. "And that's what you're planning to wear?"

She glanced down at her dress, a tiny frown wrinkling her forehead. "Yes. What's the matter? Don't you like it?"

"It just looks a little...skimpy to me. The temperature is forty degrees out and falling. A woman could catch pneumonia in a dress like that."

She smiled. "Well, I'm not too worried. I'll be driving my car, which has a wonderful heating system, and is currently parked in the heated hotel garage." Her teasing tone only made him look more grim. "I'm assuming the restaurant is heated, too, although once I give my car to the valet, I will have those four or five steps to walk to the front door of the restaurant."

The elevator dinged and the doors slid open. To her surprise, Brock followed her to the parking garage. "What time do you plan to be home?"

"If I'm lucky, I'll make it back by lunch tomorrow."

Her words brought him to a halt. She turned and gave him a wave before breezing through the door that led to her car, her cheeks warm and a delicious buzz zinging through her body. Brock was jealous! She'd never had a man react like that before. It gave her a heady feeling of feminine power and more confidence than ever about her date with Todd.

She hadn't driven a mile before her cellular phone buzzed. "Hello?"

"All right," Brock began, "maybe I was acting a little overprotective. But I've never had a sister, so I guess I came on a little too strong. With Tony in Brazil, somebody has to look out for you."

A *sister?* Her grip tightened on the cell phone. He thought of her as a sister? "You certainly haven't been kissing me like a brother," she retorted, her disappointment giving free rein to her tongue.

Silence crackled over the line. "I'm sorry about that."

Sorry about what? she wondered. The big brother routine, or kissing her? Kate decided she didn't want to know. "I need to go now."

"Wait a minute," Brock interjected. "That crack about arriving home in time for lunch tomorrow— that was just to put me in my place, wasn't it?"

That's exactly what it had been, but she wasn't about to admit it now. "I'm not sure what my plans are. It all depends on Todd."

He muttered something under his breath that she couldn't comprehend.

"Did you say something?" she asked.

"No. Have a good time, Kate." The line cut off.

She stared at the phone for a moment before setting it beside her. What right did he have to be angry? First he tries to kiss her clothes off, then he wants to play big brother. Talk about mixed signals!

"Don't think about Brock right now," she said aloud, flipping on her wipers as a light mist coated the windshield. "Just put him out of your mind."

But as persistent as the rain, Brock filled her thoughts all the way to the restaurant. She didn't understand him, but that didn't stop her from wanting him. From fantasizing about him at the most inopportune moments. Like now, standing in the foyer of the restaurant, waiting to meet the man of her dreams. She took a deep breath, wondering if it was the tight dress that made it difficult to breathe or a sudden case of the jitters.

"Kate? Kate Talavera? Is it really you?"

She turned and recognized him instantly. Todd was as blond as he looked on television, although his wavy locks had recently been tamed into a stylishly short cut. His blue eyes sparkled and he still had the same heart-stopping dimple in his chin. He walked toward her, looking better in his custom-tailored gray suit than he had in a football uniform.

She smiled and held out her hand, remembering how much she'd adored him as a teenager. "Hello, Todd."

He shook his head in amazement. "You take my breath away, Kate. I can't believe it's really you."

She silently thanked Chelsea for making her buy the dress. "It's really me. You haven't changed much at all."

He grinned that same, endearing grin that she remembered so well. "Don't let my stockholders hear you say that. They don't know I almost flunked accounting class in high school."

"You didn't almost flunk," she replied, as the maitre d' escorted them to their table. "As I remember it, you got the highest grade in the class."

"Thanks to you lending me all your class notes." He took the wine list from the maitre d', then ordered a bottle in perfect French.

She'd never been to Canlis before and was suitably impressed by both the decor and the clientele. A single candle flickered on the table between them.

"So, tell me what made you say yes tonight." Todd smiled and his teeth were so white, she wondered if they'd been capped. He'd chipped the front one in a bicycle accident when he was eight, but it looked perfect now.

She smiled back, trying to think of a witty response. According to Gwen, men lived for the thrill of the chase. The question was, now that Todd had caught her, would he want to keep her?

And did she really want him to?

The wine steward arrived, forestalling her answer. Todd took his time tasting the wine, finally nodding his approval. She wondered if her father and Brock were having fun at the bowling alley. Sid had taken Tony, Kate and Brock there once when they were younger. Brock had never been bowling before, which she'd found shocking at the time. He'd hung on to Sid's every word about how to throw the ball and approached the lane the first time with such a serious expression on his face that she and Tony had burst out laughing. Later, she and Brock had shared a basket of fried clams. Funny how she hadn't remembered all of that until now.

"I think you'll enjoy this particular year," he said, picking up his wineglass. "I've become something of a connoisseur."

She took a sip of her wine, finding it a little too sweet for her taste. "So how are your parents? They must be thrilled you've come back for a visit."

"Yes, but they're still as stubborn as ever," Todd replied. "I've been trying to talk them into moving to California for years, but they don't want to give up the old homestead."

"I can't imagine the neighborhood without them."

He nodded. "I've finally given up the argument. Who knows, maybe someday I'll decide to relocate here."

The words made her stomach flutter. Or maybe it was a reaction to the expensive wine. She normally spent three hundred dollars on things like her car payment, not a bottle of wine. She took another sip, growing more accustomed to the flavor.

"Do you mind if I take the liberty of ordering dinner for us?" he asked, opening a menu.

"Please do."

She slowly sipped her wine while he placed their order with the waiter. She wondered how a man with his charm, looks and wealth had remained single for so long. Then again, Brock was single, too, and she'd never questioned it. In fact, she rather liked the idea that no woman had led him to the altar.

"You have to tell me where you found that dynamite dress," Todd said after the waiter departed with their order. He picked up the wine bottle to refill her glass.

"In New York. I was there at Christmas for a friend's wedding."

"At Saks?" he guessed. "We do some great knock-offs of their stuff."

"Oh, you mean on your shopping channel?"

He nodded. "It's always a struggle to stay ahead of the competition. The secret is to offer the customer quality merchandise, or at least, merchandise that looks like it costs a lot of money, for a reasonable price. People are always hunting for a bargain."

"What's your most popular item?" she asked, her mind wandering back to the bowling alley. Her mom and dad used to belong to a weekly couples' league. She wondered why they didn't bowl together anymore. Maybe they had been growing apart. Kate hadn't really noticed. Obviously, her father hadn't either.

"Then we have a small inventory of loss leaders," Todd said.

She blinked, realizing she hadn't been paying attention. "Really? How interesting."

"Marketing is a lot like fishing," Todd explained. "You want to bait the hook with something the customer can't resist, then once you've got them, reel them in with the true moneymakers."

Kate managed to keep her attention on their conversation through the next three courses and learned more about the home shopping business than she ever wanted to know. By the time they finished dessert, she was hiding a yawn behind her hand.

"It's been wonderful seeing you again," Todd said, as the waiter cleared the last of their dishes away. "You look better than I ever imagined."

She smiled. "I finally figured out that the blimp look wasn't in style anymore."

"You never looked like a blimp," he countered. "I've always thought you were very pretty. Especially your beautiful brown eyes."

His words warmed her and made her feel guilty for drifting in and out of their dinner conversation. He was probably nervous, too, and thought talking about his business was the best way to fill the awkward silences.

The day had been filled with ups and downs. First the loss of the skirt, then Brock's kisses and Tony's good news about the baby. No wonder she was distracted.

"Can we do this again sometime?" he asked. "Some time very soon."

"I'd like that," Kate replied honestly.

"How about tomorrow night?"

She laughed. "That is soon."

"Please say yes."

"Yes," she replied, not giving herself time to think about it. Despite the less than scintillating dinner conversation, Todd really was perfect for her.

They walked out of the restaurant and waited near the entrance for the valet service to retrieve their cars. Kate shivered slightly, her dress not protecting her much from the cool evening breeze. She remembered Brock's warning about pneumonia and smiled to herself.

"I've had a wonderful evening, Kate." Todd took another step close to her.

She inhaled sharply, realizing a moment before it happened that he was going to kiss her.

His lips brushed against hers, soft and dry. It was just a whisper of a kiss, but something she'd dreamed about since she was fourteen years old.

After a moment, Todd pulled back and gazed into her eyes until the purr of an engine broke the spell. Her Intrepid sat idling beside them. "Your ride awaits, Cinderella."

She floated to her car, so glad she wasn't a pumpkin anymore.

12

"LOOKS LIKE you're a little off your game tonight," Sid Talavera said, adding up the final score of the bowling match. "I beat you by over forty pins."

"Must have been all those fried clams I ate," Brock said, handing Sid a ten dollar bill. "A dollar a game was our wager and you won all ten."

"So I did," Sid said with a chuckle. "I remember whenever I bowled against Rose and I was beating her, she'd start humming 'I Can't Stop Loving You' to distract me. That was the song that was playing on the car radio the first time..." He cleared his throat. "Well, never mind."

"We should have invited Rose to come with us tonight," Brock said. "I'd love to see her again."

"She's the one who left," Sid said briskly. "She's the one who has to make the first call. But I still don't understand why Katie didn't come. She loves bowling. I think they're working her too hard at that hotel."

Brock bent down to untie his bowling shoes.

"Well, actually, she had a date. With Todd Winslow."

Sid raised an eyebrow. "The Winslow boy? Rose saw him a few months ago in California. Apparently, he's done very well for himself."

"He's an egotistical jerk," Brock bit out. "Kate would be much better off without him."

"Is that a fact?" Sid folded his arms across his chest. "I know you beat the hell out of him in high school, although I still don't know why. Is this just an old grudge, or do you have good reason to think he's not right for my girl?"

A muscle flexed in Brock's jaw. "Call it a gut instinct."

Sid nodded. "I've had those before. Although, sometimes it gets confusing down there, especially when a man isn't doing his thinking with his head. Of course, you're the one who wanted to go bowling with me tonight. There was nothing stopping you from asking Katie out yourself."

"It's complicated."

"Life always is." Sid picked up his bowling bag and walked to the bar. "Since I'm the big winner tonight, I'll buy you a beer before we go."

"That seems only fair," Brock replied, placing his rented bowling shoes on the counter as he followed Sid. When they reached the bar, Brock glanced at the clock on the wall. It was fifteen minutes faster than his watch. "Do you have the time, Sid?"

"Your watch is right," Sid replied, without looking at his own. "They set them fast in here to get rid of the stragglers for last call."

"Right," Brock said, feeling like a fool. He knew about that practice. He'd been in bars all over the world, including the bar owned by Dooley, who did the same thing with his clocks.

Sid ordered two frosty mugs of beer, then turned to Brock. "Maybe you should give her a call. See how her date went."

"I don't think Kate would appreciate my interference."

"Maybe not. But it sure beats moping around like you have all night."

Brock didn't realize he'd been that obvious. "I'm not the only one who's been moping over a woman."

Sid scowled. "That's different."

"How so?"

Sid picked up his beer mug. "It just is."

"I'll make you a deal," Brock said, Sid's stubbornness giving him sudden inspiration. "I'll call Kate if you call Rose."

"And what do I say to my wife?" Sid asked. "Come home or else? What if she decides to do 'or else'?"

"You might want to phrase it a little differently. Why don't you start slow? Invite her out for a date."

Sid looked at him like he was crazy. "Date my wife?"

"Why not? When's the last time you took her out someplace nice?"

The older man shrugged. "We usually go to the sports bar down the street for the Saturday night special. All the enchiladas you can eat."

"No, I mean someplace romantic," Brock clarified. "Candles. Violin music. Linen napkins."

"Beats me."

"Kate was going to Canlis tonight. You should have seen her, Sid. She was a knockout. Imagine giving Rose a chance to get all dressed up like that. You could wear a suit and tie, pick her up in your car. Even bring along a cassette tape of 'I Can't Stop Loving You' to play in the tape deck. Who knows where it might lead?"

Sid rubbed his chin between his fingers. "You know, that might not be a bad idea."

Brock pulled his cell phone out of his pocket. "All you have to do is make the call."

TWO HOURS LATER, Brock was pacing back and forth in front of Kate's hotel room. It was almost two o'clock in the morning and she still wasn't back from her date yet.

Or maybe she was. Maybe she had Winslow in her room at this moment. In her bed. He stopped short, his gut churning at the thought. If she did, there wasn't a damn thing he could do about it.

He turned and made his way slowly to the elevator. He pressed the button, then watched the floor lights flash above the door as the elevator car slowly ascended to the third floor.

The doors slid open and Kate stood inside, along with an elderly couple.

She blinked up at him in surprise. "We've got to stop meeting like this."

Relief washed over him. She was home. And she was alone. "I wanted to talk to you about your folks."

"At two in the morning?" She stepped out of the elevator, followed by the elderly couple, who took off down the long hallway. The elevator doors closed behind her. "Have you been waiting outside my room all this time?"

"I just got here," he said, mentally condensing the last two hours into a few minutes. "I thought you'd be back by now."

"Actually, I got back a couple of hours ago. I've been working in my office."

His mood lightened considerably. "Really?"

"Really. Now what's going on with my parents? Good news, I hope."

"The best. They have a dinner date tomorrow night."

Her face brightened. "That's wonderful!"

"I talked your dad into taking Rose to Canlis. He called her and she said yes."

"Oh, Brock." She threw her arms around him. "Thank you so much!"

He held her close, savoring the maddening scent of her perfume. His body instantly hardened at the contact of her breasts against his chest. He wanted to pick her up in his arms and carry her to his room. Keep her there, in his bed, until he'd driven Todd Winslow and every other man she'd ever met completely out of her mind.

She stepped away from him before he could put his impulsive plan into action. "I'm so happy. I'll call Mom tomorrow and invite her to the hotel's spa for the full treatment. Manicure, pedicure, facial—the works."

His gaze fell to the rapid rise and fall of her chest. The dress revealed the tops of her creamy breasts and his mouth suddenly ached to taste them. He licked his lips. "Sounds like a great idea."

"I don't know how to thank you."

He could think of a million ways. Or just one. One perfect night with Kate Talavera in his arms. "You don't have to thank me. Let's see if it works first."

"It will work. It has to."

"How was your date?"

She hesitated. "Nice. Very nice."

"Are you free tomorrow night?" he asked impulsively. "Ever since we talked to Carla Corona, I've been thinking about trying one of those ferry rides."

Her face fell. "Oh. Brock, I'm sorry. I already have plans."

His jaw clenched. "With Winslow?"

"Yes."

"I see. Well, good night, Kate." He pushed the elevator button again.

She hesitated. "Good night." Then she walked toward her room.

He knew he was acting like a jerk. She had a right to date any man she wanted, even Winslow. Besides, describing a date as *nice* gave him room to hope. As did the lack of enthusiasm in her voice. Maybe Scumbag would implode the relationship all on his own, without any outside help from him.

The sound of Kate's voice crying out made him turn and look down the length of the hallway. He saw her standing in front of her door, a look of horror on her face. He ran toward her as fast as his legs would carry him. One of the security guards who made the rounds each night got there at the same time.

"What's wrong?" Brock asked. But she didn't have to tell him. He could see the condition of the room for himself. The furniture had been turned upside down, the pictures torn off the walls. The small kitchenette had been ransacked, too. The drawers pulled out and the contents spread over the floor. All the cupboard doors hung wide open, boxes and canned goods spilled all over the counter.

Kate wrapped her arms around herself. "Who would do something like this?"

The security guard clicked on his radio and gave orders to contact the police. Then he checked out the room to make certain the intruder had left.

"It's clear," the guard said, ushering them inside. "I'll go down to the lobby and wait for the police. The less commotion we can cause, the better for our guests. Please try not to touch anything."

The next moment, they were alone, although the intruder's presence still permeated the room.

"I don't understand it." Her voice sounded tight and strained. "Who would do something like this? There's no money here. No valuables."

Except the skirt. Brock surveyed the damage. "Do you think anything is missing?" he asked.

She did a quick check of the room, then walked into her bedroom and came out again a few moments later. "As far as I can tell, everything is still here. Why didn't the burglar take the television set? Or the microwave?"

Brock was afraid he knew the answer. Because this

burglar was looking for something very specific—the skirt. Dooley had told him they'd had more than one inquiry about it. Had the other potential client hired someone else's services to do the job? The thought made him sick inside. If it was true, then Kate was possibly in danger.

"Is it cold in here?" she asked, rubbing her hands up and down her bare arms.

Brock slipped off his jacket and placed it over her shoulders, then led her over to the sofa. "You've had a shock. It's a natural reaction."

"I suppose you're right," she said, shivering slightly. "I've never been the victim of a crime before. I had no idea it felt like this."

He circled one arm around her and pulled her closer. "Give it some time. You'll feel better soon."

She turned to look at him. "How can you be so sure? Has something like this ever happened to you before?"

He tenderly brushed a stray curl off her forehead. "Once or twice. In my line of work, you cross paths with all sorts of people."

She shook her head in disbelief. "I hope nothing like this ever happens again."

"It won't," he said firmly. "I promise."

A shadow of a smile teased her lips. "How can you possibly keep a promise like that?"

"Because I won't let it happen. I want you to come to my room tonight. You can't stay here."

She shook her head. "No. I won't be chased out of here. I'll be fine."

"If you won't come to my room, then I'm staying here with you. I'll sleep on the sofa."

"You can't stay with me forever." She looked into his eyes. "Can you?"

He hesitated, not certain what she wanted him to say. "I'll stay until you feel safe again."

She leaned back against the sofa and took a deep breath. He didn't know if those were the words she wanted to hear, but his own mind was spinning. How could he have let this happen? Had his attraction to Kate made him lose his focus? Were there clues he should have seen? Hints that someone else was on the hunt for the skirt?

Twenty minutes later, a policeman arrived to make a report, along with a lab technician who dusted for fingerprints. But Brock's experience told him the job had been done by a professional. They wouldn't find any significant prints in the room other than Kate's and his own.

"Thank you, officer," Kate said, when the interview concluded. The lab technician had packed up his bag and was waiting for the cop by the door. "Please let me know if you find out who did this. And why."

The cop nodded. "We'll do our best, ma'am. Give us a call if you discover anything missing."

"I will."

Once they were gone, Kate closed the door and bolted it. Then she turned to face Brock, faint purple shadows under her eyes.

"You should be in bed," he said. "You look exhausted."

"Care to join me?" she asked softly. The words were out of her mouth before she had time to think about it. But she didn't want to take them back. She wanted Brock. For now—for as long as he could give her.

That's when it hit her. She'd been rationalizing her attraction to him ever since he'd seen her wearing the skirt. *But maybe it was meant to happen.* Maybe fate had arranged that chance meeting between them at her parents' house. Maybe it was time to stop fighting her feelings and surrender to the need for him that was now pounding in her veins. To follow her heart instead of her head.

She just hoped it wasn't too late. It had been over a week since Brock had seen her in the skirt. Perhaps the effect had worn off.

Brock hadn't moved since her invitation. She took a step toward him and saw his entire body tense. "Well?"

He cleared his throat, but his voice still sounded

husky when he spoke. "I don't think that's a good idea."

It had taken all of Kate's courage to come this far. She wasn't about to give up so easily. "Maybe I can change your mind."

She heard Brock's quick intake of breath as she leaned up to kiss him. Her hand curled around his neck as her tongue teased his lips. His mouth opened to let her inside as a low groan rumbled from deep in his chest.

The fingers of her other hand crept up the front of his shirt, slipping each button free of its hole. Then her palm splayed over his bare chest, right above his heart. Another groan tore from his throat as her hands tugged his shirt out of his jeans and pushed it off his shoulders. Pressing her body against him, she kissed a tender spot right under his jaw.

Brock heard a roaring in his ears as the blood pounded in his veins. He was on the razor's edge of losing control. "Kate, we have to stop."

"Why?" she whispered, letting his shirt drop soundlessly to the floor.

Why? How could he possibly answer that question or any question with all the blood draining from his head and pooling low in his body. His groin pulsed with urgent need for her.

She lowered her head and dropped tantalizing kisses on his chest, her tongue flicking out to taste each flat nipple. "Do you want me, Brock?" she asked softly.

He closed his eyes at her words. The scent of her drove him crazy and he wanted to see all of her. Had to see all of her. He circled one finger along the bodice of her dress, making it gape open far enough to reveal the erect pink tips of her creamy breasts. He pulled her down on the sofa, his hands tugging the red silk down low enough to free her breasts so he could taste them. He took his time, savoring the experience.

Her head dropped back, her eyelids fluttering shut as he circled and palmed and sucked first one breast, then the other. She twined her slender fingers through his hair as her soft cries of desire filled his ears.

His conscience battled with his desire as he felt her fingers fumble with the fly of his jeans. *Stop.* No, he thought, fiercely. He couldn't stop. Not now. Not after he'd wanted her for so long. But did she really want him? Or did she just need something to block out the shock and the fear of the break-in?

He wanted her. Wanted her desperately. But not like this. Not when she might need him for so many reasons but the right one. For security. For comfort. For confidence. She'd made it clear she wanted Winslow, so why this sudden change of heart? Had the jerk hurt her in some way? Shaken her confidence? Whatever the reason, Brock didn't want to be the consolation prize.

What if he made love to her and she regretted it in the morning? That thought cleared his lust-clouded brain. He pulled away from her, though his body throbbed in protest. He couldn't do this. Not to himself. Not to Kate.

She half-sat up, her breathing fast and heavy. Her dress was crumpled below her bare breasts. "What's wrong?"

"We can't do this." He stood up and turned away from her, buttoning the fly of his jeans with difficulty and trying to steady his breathing. "*I* can't do this. Not now."

"Oh." She blanched, then hastily pulled up her dress, trying to cover herself. "I'm sorry. I didn't mean to throw myself at you. I guess I'm a little frazzled by everything that's happened." Her cheeks turned almost as red as her dress.

"Don't apologize. It's my fault. I never should have taken advantage of you."

"If I remember right, I'm the one who asked you to spend the night with me." She stood up, still holding the dress clasped to her chest. "Don't worry. It won't happen again." Then she escaped into the bedroom and closed the door behind her. A moment later, he heard the click of the deadbolt.

"Damn." Brock dropped back down to the sofa, rubbing his face with his hands. When had he lost control of this mission?

When had he fallen in love with Kate Talavera?

13

WHEN BROCK AWOKE on the sofa the next morning, he was surprised to find Kate already gone. Her bed was neatly made and she'd picked up all the debris from the night before and straightened the furniture.

He padded to the kitchenette and made himself a cup of instant coffee. His shirt still lay on the floor where Kate had dropped it last night. If he hadn't stopped her, they might be in her bed together right now. Why the hell had he suddenly decided to become noble?

Taking a sip of his coffee, Brock walked over to the table and sat down, then punched out Dooley's number on his cellular phone. He hoped the old guy was still an early riser.

"Dooley, here," barked a deep voice on the other end of the line.

"It's Brock," he said, leaning one elbow on the table. "I need a favor."

"All you have to do is name it."

"I want to know who else is looking for the skirt."

"Have you got competition?"

"Possibly."

Dooley sighed over the line. "The other guy didn't give me a name. He just made the one call, then I never heard from him again. Is he causing trouble?"

"He, or she, left a calling card last night. Kate's hotel room was ripped apart."

"So what's the status of the skirt?"

"I have it secured," Brock told him. "But I'm not about to leave until I know Kate is safe. And the only way to know that is to find out who else wants the skirt."

"Who do you suspect?" Dooley asked.

"It looks like a professional hit. Maybe the Gunderson boys. They tend to get messy. Or possibly the Weasel. It was a thorough job. I'm just damn glad they came up empty-handed."

"Me, too," Dooley replied. "I'll start nosing around and see what I can find out."

Brock knew the man would come up with something. He always did. "Thanks, Dooley."

"Don't thank me," Dooley said. "I've got my own selfish reasons for wanting your butt back in Boston."

"Another job?"

"That's right. A big one, too. Down in Rio. They want my best man and that's you, Brock."

"I may be here awhile yet," he replied, feeling none of the old anticipation at the prospect of a challenging mission. "At least another few days. Maybe more."

"If you have the skirt, why the delay?"

"I told you about the break-in."

"And," Dooley prodded, his finely honed instincts obviously kicking in.

"And I told Kate I was here for her parents' anniversary party. I'm going to stay at least that long. I've told her enough lies already."

Dooley didn't say anything.

"Can you send Bryant to Rio?" Brock suggested. "He's good. Very good."

"You don't want the job?"

Brock hesitated. "I don't know what I want anymore."

Dooley's voice lost its familiar hard edge. "Maybe you'd better stay in Seattle until you figure it out."

After Brock hung up, he finished the rest of his coffee, then headed to his own hotel room. The first thing he did was check under the bed, where he'd taped the package containing the skirt. Then he jumped in the shower, making it a cold one to drive all thoughts of Kate from his mind.

It didn't work.

He was rubbing the towel over his head when the telephone rang. He picked it up, hoping it was Kate. "Hello?"

"Brock, this is Sid. You've got to get over here. It's an emergency."

His hair was still wet when he pulled into the Talavera driveway. Sid met him at the door.

"What's the problem?" Brock asked, certain the house had suffered a break-in last night, too.

"My suit doesn't fit."

"What?" Brock followed Sid into the living room. He saw a pair of dark brown slacks draped across the sofa. A matching suit jacket lay crumpled on the coffee table.

"I dug it out of the closet to wear for my date with Rose tonight and the damn thing doesn't fit!" Sid raked a hand through his gray hair. "It's too small. I know it's been awhile since I wore it, but I can't even button the damn jacket."

"Don't panic," Brock told him. "There's a simple solution to this problem. Women have been doing it for centuries."

"Dieting?" Sid ventured.

"Shopping."

"THIS IS RIDICULOUS," Rose Talavera said. "Paraffin wax is used to seal homemade jam, not for smearing all over your face."

She and Kate reclined side-by-side in salon chairs. They'd spent most of the afternoon having various parts of their bodies buffed and polished. The hotel's spa was famous for its facials, but Rose obviously wasn't impressed.

"How much did you say this cost again?"

"It doesn't matter," Kate replied, feeling her pores tighten under the mask. "It's my treat."

"Your father probably won't even recognize me by the time I leave this place." Rose heaved a long sigh. "Maybe that will be a good thing."

"Remember, Mom, you're supposed to think only positive thoughts." Kate had been trying hard to follow her own advice. She'd been mortified when Brock had rejected her last night, but in the light of day she realized maybe he'd been right. If her room hadn't been ransacked, she never would have attacked him like that. She'd simply wanted to forget. To lose herself in Brock's arms.

But even now, while her brain was telling her one thing, her body was remembering how his mouth had worshipped her breasts and a delicious tingle shot down to her toes.

"Isn't it funny that we both have dates tonight?" Rose mused beside her.

"Oh. Yes." Kate had forgotten all about Todd. That was becoming a bad habit. Especially since she'd been able to think of little else before Brock had come into town.

Her esthetician began to peel off Kate's mask while another one worked on Rose.

"Where's Todd taking you tonight?" Rose asked.

"I don't really know. He sent me another two dozen red roses today and the card said he'd pick me up at eight."

Rose sniffed. "Maybe Todd should give your father a couple of pointers about romance."

"You never know, Mom," Kate said. She closed her eyes, hoping Brock could do the impossible and turn her no-nonsense father into a late-blooming Casanova.

"EIGHT HUNDRED DOLLARS?" Sid exclaimed, loud enough to cause several patrons of the Butch Blum store to turn and stare. "You want me to spend eight hundred dollars on *one* suit? I already spent twenty-five dollars on a corsage and fifty dollars on cologne." He shook his head. "At this rate, I'll have to take out a bank loan before I ask my wife out for a second date."

"You want to make a good impression on Rose, don't you?" Brock asked, folding his arms across his chest. He'd spent the past three hours shopping for a suit for Sid, who was pickier about his clothes than any woman could ever be. Either the pants were too short or the sleeves were too long. And they didn't have time for alterations. Now they'd finally found the perfect one and the man was balking at the price tag.

"I could buy five suits down at a discount store for eight hundred dollars. Don't you think that would impress Rose even more?"

The clerk who had been helping them stepped forward to brush a wrinkle out of the shoulder pad on Sid's coat. "Take a look in the mirror, Mr. Talavera. This suit makes you look twenty years younger."

"You're paid on commission, aren't you?" Sid asked, tugging at the tie around his neck.

"I'd say you look about twenty pounds lighter, too," Brock added, glancing at his watch. "You're due to meet Rose at the Canlis restaurant in less than an hour, so you'd better make a decision."

Sid turned and looked at his reflection in the long mirror, straightening the lapel of the gray pinstripe jacket. "You really think Rose will like it?"

"I'd bet money on it," Brock replied.

"I don't have any money left to wager," Sid replied. "Although, I guess if it doesn't work, I could always return the suit tomorrow for a refund."

The clerk raised an eyebrow.

"Don't worry," Sid assured him, checking out the view from the rear. "I won't order spaghetti or red wine, or anything that could leave a stain."

Brock bit back a smile. "If you're lucky, you'll have lipstick stains all over that suit before the night is over."

Sid turned to the clerk. "I'll take it."

AT PRECISELY seven o'clock that evening, Kate hunched down behind the steering wheel of her Intrepid in the parking lot of the Canlis restaurant. She could see her mother waiting by the front entrance, patting down her new hairstyle and smoothing down the silk skirt of her new dress.

She heard her father's old Dodge pickup truck before she saw it, the worn-out muffler announcing his arrival. He pulled up to the front entrance, climbed out of the cab and tossed his keys to the valet. She hardly recognized him in his new suit. A moment later, she saw her mother's eyes widen in appreciation.

"Easy on the gas pedal," Sid called out, as the valet attempted to shift the sputtering truck into gear. "It tends to stick a little. And don't fiddle with the radio. I've got it tuned just right."

Kate watched as her father turned to face Rose. They both avoided making direct eye contact and she wished she could hear what they were saying.

Suddenly, the passenger door of Kate's car opened and Brock slid inside. "Guess I'm not the only one nervous about this date tonight. Are you spying, too?"

"Of course," she said, avoiding his gaze. The last time she'd seen him they had both been half-dressed. All day, she'd wondered what she'd say when she saw him again. Now he was here, in her car, and looking sexier than ever.

"Sid put on so much cologne, that valet will probably asphyxiate in the pickup cab."

Kate turned to him, putting last night out of her mind. "I don't know how to thank you for talking Dad into making this date. I've never seen Mom so excited."

"Glad to help." Brock cocked his head to one side. "I thought you had a date with Winslow tonight."

"I do," she replied. "But not for another hour."

His gaze skittered over the black sheath dress she wore, lingering just long enough to make her skin prickle. "Looks nice. And a lot warmer than what you had on last night."

His words instantly brought back the way he'd last seen her, with the red dress pushed down to her waist, her breasts bared, her nipples moist from his tongue. She cleared her throat and stared straight ahead, glad it was too dark for him to see her blush.

"Mom promised to call me when she gets in tonight," Kate said, hastily changing the subject, "and tell me how the date went."

"I told Sid to do the same thing. After they do, we can compare notes."

"I might not be back from my date when she calls," Kate clarified. "She told me she'd leave a message on my machine."

"That won't be necessary. I'll be there to answer your phone."

Kate shook her head. "*That* won't be necessary. I appreciate your concern, but the hotel has beefed up security. And I can take care of myself. I've been doing a pretty good job for the past twenty-seven years."

"Don't argue with me about this, Kate. You're not going to win."

But she wasn't about to give in. "How will it look when Todd brings me home tonight if you're in my room waiting up for me?"

His jaw tightened. "You're planning to bring Winslow to your room?"

She switched on the ignition, not about to discuss her love life with Brock. Not after the way he had declined to be a part of it last night. "I need to go."

"You deserve someone better than Winslow," he said, his voice low and tight.

"Well, since men aren't exactly standing in line to sweep me off my feet, I'll take my chances with Todd."

"He's an asshole."

She jerked her head toward him. "Maybe he's changed in the past twelve years. You certainly have."

"So have you." Brock reached out to grasp her arm. "Don't settle for a man like Winslow. He's shallow and selfish. A taker, not a giver. Always has been."

She pulled away from him. "I'm not going to let your old grudge against the man affect my relationship with him. You never liked him, Brock. Admit it."

"I never even noticed him until..." His voice trailed off and he looked out the window.

"Until what?" she prodded, waiting to hear a valid reason to dump Todd. "Until he made starting quarterback of the football team? Until he was voted class president?"

"He was two years behind me in high school," Brock said between his teeth. "So I could care less about his so-called accomplishments. I just didn't happen to like the way he treated women."

"And I already told you that I don't need another big brother."

He stared at her, then without another word, climbed out of her car and shut the door. She screeched out of the parking lot, watching him in her rearview mirror. He didn't look happy.

Good. That made two of them.

14

"THANK YOU AGAIN for a wonderful evening," Todd murmured, taking a step closer to her.

"I should be thanking you." They stood outside Kate's hotel room door and she was torn as to whether she should invite him inside. It had been a magical evening, beginning with a scenic twilight drive around Lake Washington, then followed by an intimate dinner for two at the cozy Leschi Lake Cafe.

It would have been the perfect date if Brock Gannon hadn't kept intruding her thoughts. How dare he act the part of the jealous lover? And what right did he have to tell Kate who she could or couldn't date? Especially when he wasn't volunteering.

"You've been driving me crazy all night," Todd said, cupping her chin in his hand. The look in his eyes told her he was going to kiss her again. She took a deep breath, inhaling his expensive cologne.

He leaned forward and grazed his lips over her mouth. They were soft and dry, like his hands. A lusty moan sounded in his throat. She found herself comparing his technique to the way Brock had kissed her last night. Todd's kiss was tamer. Less heated. Nice.

There's nothing wrong with nice, Kate told herself, as Todd deepened the kiss. His tongue sought entrance inside her mouth as he leaned into her.

The momentum caused her to step backward, her elbow bumping against the door. The next moment the door flew open and Kate had to grab Todd's arms to keep from falling backward.

"I'm sorry," Brock said, not sounding the least bit contrite. "I thought I heard someone knock."

Todd stared at him for a moment, then recognition dawned. "Gannon," he said, his mouth turning down in a frown. "What are you doing here?"

"I need to talk to Kate."

"I'm busy right now," she replied, furious with him for showing up in her hotel suite when she had specifically asked him not to.

Brock's eyes hardened. "This can't wait."

Four teenage girls in bathing suits walked down the hallway and past the suite, their wide-eyed stares making it obvious that they'd noticed the tangible animosity between the two men. Kate had no desire to make this a public spectacle.

"Please come in, Todd," she said, brushing past Brock and walking into the room.

Todd followed her, then turned to Gannon. "Haven't you ever heard that three's a crowd?"

"As a matter of fact, I have. Feel free to leave anytime."

"Todd is staying," Kate said firmly, pointing a finger at Brock. "You're going."

He stood with his feet planted wide apart, imitating a brick wall. "Not until I tell you who broke into your room last night."

Kate's body tensed. "Did the police call?"

"No. But I made some inquiries." He nodded toward Todd. "You can thank Winslow here, for turning your hotel room upside down."

She looked at Todd, noticing the mottled flush on his cheeks. But was it from anger or embarrassment? "I don't understand."

"Tell her, Winslow," Brock said, folding his arms across his chest. "Tell her why you're really here."

Todd stabbed a finger in Brock's direction. "I don't have to tell you a damn thing."

Brock turned to Kate. "He knows about the skirt and he wants to use it as a marketing tool to sell cheap knockoffs on his home shopping show."

Todd took a menacing step toward Brock. "You don't know what the hell you're talking about."

Kate didn't know what to think. She sat down, her knees a little shaky. She didn't want to believe Brock, but Todd wasn't exactly denying it.

Brock ignored him, keeping his attention on Kate. "He's been romancing the skirt. That's why he's been sending you all those e-mails and flooding your room with flowers and falling all over himself to date you. It's all been a big act."

"Todd," she asked, looking up at him. "Is any of this true?"

Todd turned to her, his fists clenched. Then he took a deep breath and walked toward her. "I'll be honest with you. I know about the skirt, Kate. My researchers have been following the story ever since they read about it in the New York papers. It was their idea to embark on a marketing blitz featuring the real skirt."

Brock pulled open the door. "I think it's time for you to leave, Winslow."

Todd ignored him. He knelt beside her, his blue eyes wide and entreating. "It's true that the reason I accepted the party invitation was to make contact with you again. But I enjoyed your e-mails so much that I put off making an offer on the skirt. I knew I wanted to see you again—see if we might have a chance together."

"Get out, Winslow," Brock growled. "Now."

Todd grabbed her hand, squeezing tightly. "Once I saw you, I forgot all about the skirt. It's you I want, Kate. Only you."

He sounded sincere, but did she dare believe him? "Just answer me one question. Did you hire someone to break into my hotel suite?"

He hesitated. "Yes. No. I mean, a few weeks ago my assistant manager contacted a private agency about acquiring the skirt, but I had no idea they'd use illegal tactics."

"Was it the Gunderson Agency?" Brock asked.

Todd turned toward him, surprise etched on his face. "Yes. How did you know?"

"It's my business to know. The Gunderson boys like to leave their mark. I'm just glad Kate wasn't here when they showed up. Or did you plan it that way when you asked her out to dinner last night?"

"No. It was all a mistake." Todd's mouth thinned as he turned back to Kate. "The agency's been fired and I swear nothing like this will ever happen to you again. And I absolutely insist on paying for any damages."

Brock snorted. "You always were a slick talker, Winslow."

Todd whirled on him. "Why are you still here? Kate and I would like some privacy."

Brock took a menacing step toward him. "You want to try and make me leave?"

"Hold it," Kate exclaimed, rising to her feet. "There's something you should know, Todd. The skirt is gone. Forever. I don't have it anymore."

Todd turned to her. "Fine. Because I don't even care about the skirt anymore. That's what I've been trying to tell you."

"I need some time to think," she said, her mind spinning. "Alone."

He nodded. "I'll call you tomorrow. I hope you'll still be my date for the party." He hesitated, his eyes searching her face. "Please, Kate. Believe me."

"Goodbye, Winslow," Brock said.

Todd didn't even look at him as he turned around and walked out the open door.

Brock pushed the door shut. "It's about time he left."

"How dare you?" Kate said, her voice high and trembling with indignation. Anger and resentment burned like a white hot ember deep inside of her. "How dare you lurk in my room and spy on me?"

He frowned. "You're mad at *me*?"

"Do you deny it?" she asked. "You knew Todd and I were right outside the suite. You must have been listening at the door to open it so quickly. My elbow barely tapped it. Were you watching us through the peephole? Getting a cheap thrill?"

"Watching Winslow maul you hardly gave me a thrill." His nostrils flared. "I thought you might like to know the real reason he's been sniffing around you."

"Thank you for putting it so crudely." She tipped up her chin. "I suppose it's impossible for him to be interested in me for me alone. Is that what you're saying?"

"Of course not." A muscle flexed in his jaw. "I just thought you should know the man has ulterior motives. You can't trust him."

Kate reached up to rub her temple. She knew Brock might have a point, but that didn't mean she appreciated him doing his best to try to alienate Todd—one of the few eligible bachelors left in the world. "He sounded sincere to me. And even if you're right about his motives, maybe he really doesn't care about the skirt anymore. He didn't even blink an eyelash when I told him it was gone."

Brock moved toward her, grasping her shoulders. "Are you nuts?"

"No." She shrugged out of his hold. "I'm old enough to make my own decisions. If you want to know the truth, I'm glad the skirt is gone. At least if Todd does want me, I'll know it's because of me, and not because of some magical thread in an island skirt."

Brock looked at her long and hard. Then he turned on his heel and walked out of the room.

Her mouth fell open as she stared at the open door. Then she marched after him. "Where are you going?"

"Leave me alone, Kate." He strode past the elevator to the fire stairs, flinging the door open and taking the steps down to the second floor two at a time.

She followed him, her high heels impeding her

progress. "Not until I make myself perfectly clear. I don't want you interfering in my life anymore, Brock Gannon. Do you understand?"

He flew through the door leading to the second-floor hallway, leaving her talking to herself in the empty stairwell. His superior attitude only infuriated her more. How dare he invade her room, call her crazy, then just walk off before she was through talking to him!

"Brock," she called out, hurrying down the hallway. She saw him pull his plastic keycard from his pocket and slip it into the lock.

He muttered an oath and tried it again. She reached him just in time to see the light on the lock mechanism flash from red to green.

"Hold it," she said, grabbing his arm to keep him from escaping into his hotel room.

He stared down at her hand. "Let go of me, Kate."

His muscles grew taut beneath her palm. She was aware of a strange tension emanating from him, but she'd come too far to back down now. "Not until you tell me why you're so intent on ruining my relationship with Todd."

"Don't push this."

"Give me a reason," she persisted. "One reason why I should listen to you."

"Just one reason?" He opened the door and pulled her inside. A small lamp glowed on a corner table, illuminating the king-size bed standing in the center of the room. Unlike her suite, this room was small. Intimate.

"Okay, how about this," he said, turning to face her. "I want you when I wake up in the morning. I want you when I go to bed every night. And the wanting just gets worse in between."

She licked her dry lips. "That's just because you saw me in the skirt."

He slowly shook his head, his gaze never leaving her face. "It's not the skirt. It's you, Kate. Your beautiful eyes. Your luscious mouth. The sound of your laugh. I ran away just now because I knew I couldn't be with you another moment and not touch you."

She swallowed at the predatory expression on his face. Every nerve ending in her body came alive as he stepped toward her.

"Well, I'm tired of being noble." He moved closer still, cupping her face in his hands. "And as you can see, I'm not running anymore."

She swallowed, her throat parched. "What exactly are you saying?"

"I'm saying your body sets me on fire every time I see you. I'm saying I've never wanted anyone as much as I want you."

Before she could respond, he kissed her, pulling her against him as his mouth seared her own. His kiss was anything but nice. It was hot and frantic and full of yearning.

His tongue stroked the seam of her lips until she opened for him, their moans of pleasure blending together. She leaned into him, savoring the hardness of his body. His fingers slid over her cheeks and tangled in her hair. Red hot desire shot through her veins and she grabbed his shoulders to keep her balance.

When he finally broke the kiss, she was gasping for air, her whole body alive and tingling.

"There's one more reason you should know," he said huskily. "I'm in love with you."

"Brock, I..."

But he stopped her words with another kiss. More tender now, as he caressed her lips with his own. Seeking something she desperately wanted to give him.

Her hands slid down to his waist, then slipped under his sweater, relishing the warmth of his skin against her fingertips. They trickled through the hair on his chest, the muscles contracting beneath her touch.

Brock's hands found the zipper on the back of her dress, his mouth still clinging to hers. He slid the zipper down, the sound causing a strange sensation deep in her belly. Then he pulled the straps off her

shoulders and took a step back, causing the dress to
fall to the floor.

With his eyes locked on her face, he reached out to
undo the front clasp of her black satin bra, letting it
gape open. Then he cupped her breasts with his
hands, kneading and molding them until they filled
his palms.

"Tell me to stop," he said huskily, his hands still
moving, "and I will."

She didn't say a word. Instead, she closed her eyes
and let her head tip back, enjoying the exquisite sensation. He knew how to touch her just right. To tease
and to tempt until all she wanted to do was beg for
more. She opened her mouth to do just that, but he'd
obviously read her mind because he picked her up in
his arms and carried her to the bed.

Wrapping her arms around his neck, she savored
the delicious strength of him. She wanted to feel that
strength around her, inside of her. She wanted to
make him lose the iron control that always surrounded him.

He laid her gently on the quilted blue bedspread,
then walked over to the drapes and pulled them
open. "I want to see you. All of you." Silvery moon-
light streamed over her body. He walked over to the
nightstand and pulled a square foil package out of
the drawer. Then he pulled out a second one, laying
them both on top of the nightstand.

"It's your turn," she said huskily, sitting up to watch as he slowly pulled his sweater over his head. His jeans came off next, revealing slim hips, strong, broad thighs and long legs. Then his hands moved to the waistband of his boxer shorts.

"Let me," she said, reaching for his hand. He let her pull him to the bed and his eyelids fluttered shut as she slowly slid his boxer shorts down over his hips. Then she leaned forward and kissed the wash-board ripples above his navel. Her tongue flicked out to taste his salt-sweet skin, then moved lower.

He groaned aloud and gently pushed her back on the bed, hovering over her. "You don't know what you do to me, Kate."

She circled her arms around his neck and pulled him down on top of her. Their lips met, fitting as per-fectly together as their bodies. Mouth to mouth, skin to skin, heartbeat to heartbeat.

He lifted his head far enough to kiss the tip of her chin, nibble the corner of her mouth, and draw his tongue along the length of one eyebrow. His body was hot and hard against hers, with only her black satin panties separating them.

Brock rolled onto his side, leaning up on one el-bow. He lifted his hand and let his fingers trail lightly down the length of her neck, over her collarbone and around her breasts. He used his thumb and forefin-ger to trace and pluck the swollen nipple of her left breast, then did the same to her right, until she squirmed on the bed with longing.

Then his tongue took over, while his fingers continued their sensual assault down the length of her body, drifting over her ribs and abdomen. Delicious shivers of pleasure shot through her. When he reached her panties, he slid his palm over the smooth, satin fabric, making her hips arch up to meet him.

"Brock," she pleaded. "Please."

He lifted his mouth from her breast, his gray eyes molten with desire. "Not yet, love."

The rhythmic movement of his hand over her most intimate, sensitive place drove her wild. Her breath caught in her throat as she spiraled higher and higher. Then she felt a cool draft of air below her waist and realized her panties were gone.

She reached up to touch him, tracing her hand along the ridge of his biceps, over one broad shoulder, then curving it around his neck to pull him to her for another long, simmering kiss. She rocked against him. Once. Twice.

His hand curled around her bare hip and pulled her underneath him, making her gasp at the intimate contact of their bodies. He was incredibly hot. Incredibly hard. So very ready for her.

"Kate," he gasped, his breathing heavy and harsh. "I can't wait any longer."

He leaned up toward the nightstand, then she heard the rip of foil. The next moment he was on top of her again, his gray eyes stormy with desire. "I want you so much."

She wrapped her legs around his waist, urging him onward. He joined her with a guttural groan of satisfaction, filling her with the promise of ecstasy.

Then he began to move and she closed her eyes with a moan of surrender, letting him take her to a place she'd never been before. She lost all sense of time, not certain if minutes or hours had passed when she heard his hoarse shout of satisfaction mingle with her own cries of fulfillment.

Brock dropped on top of her, his naked body slick with perspiration. "I love you, Kate," he growled into her hair. "I love you."

She closed her eyes and smiled, her body sated. After all this time, she'd finally found him. Brock Gannon—her friend, her lover, her future.

The man she'd been waiting for all her life.

15

"MMMM, YOU TASTE GOOD."

Kate opened her eyes the next morning to find Brock laying beside her, nibbling at her neck. "Hungry?" she asked with a smile.

"Starving." He pulled her on top of him until she sat straddling his hips. He was more than ready for her.

She fit herself to him, enjoying the position to watch the play of expressions on his face. Then she began to move. They made slow, languorous love, Brock letting her set the pace.

It was even better than the night before.

Afterward, she lay cradled in his arms, her hand splayed across his chest. "Still hungry?"

"Ravenous," he leaning over to kiss the tip of her breast. "But I suppose I'll have to settle for breakfast this time."

"Shall I order room service?"

"Sounds good." He stretched out beside her, folding his hands behind his head.

She reached for the telephone. "First I want to

check my messages. I can't wait to hear how Mom and Dad's date turned out."

"I'm surprised your Dad didn't call me last night." Brock smiled. "Maybe he was occupied."

She dialed her answering service, then retrieved the message from her mother. The tone of Rose's voice made her frown.

"Bad news?" Brock asked, stroking one hand over her bare back.

She disconnected the line. "According to Mom, their date started out fine. Then Dad told her it was time for her to move back home, she told him it was time for him to retire, and the evening went down hill from there."

He leaned up to kiss her shoulder. "So now what?"

She sighed. "Well, the party's tonight, so we're running out of options. I'm going to call each of them and ask them to meet me at the Harbor Room in the hotel at 7:30 p.m. All the guests will be there by then."

"Do you think that's a good idea?"

"Who knows?" She sighed as he lifted her hair up to kiss the back of her neck. "Maybe being surrounded by all their old friends and reliving old memories will bring them back together again."

He looked doubtful. "I suppose it's worth a shot."

"Do you have any other suggestions?"

"A few," he kissed her other shoulder. "But they have nothing to do with your parents."

She smiled as his mouth moved to the side of her neck. "I thought you wanted breakfast."

"Among other things," he said, then nipped her earlobe before rising out of bed and walking to the bathroom.

She settled back against the pillows to enjoy the view. "How do you like your eggs?"

"Naked in bed with you," he said, turning at the door. "Do you mind if I shower first?"

"Go ahead." She dialed room service and placed an order for two. When she hung up, she could hear the sound of the shower running behind the closed bathroom door and Brock's deep voice belting out a tuneless rendition of "I Can't Stop Loving You."

Kate smiled to herself as she stretched her arms over her head, more content than she'd ever been in her life. The scent of their lovemaking drifted up from the sheets as she swung her legs over the side of the bed and searched the floor for her panties.

She saw a scrap of black peeking out from under the bed and reached for it. But it wasn't her panties. It was a loose strip of duct tape. She kneeled on the carpet for a closer look, surprised to find the duct tape connected to a plastic bag that was attached to the underside of the bed.

"What in the world?" she muttered, pulling the

rest of the tape loose. She'd learned in her profession that hotel guests did all kinds of strange things. No doubt someone had decided it would be safer to tape their valuables under the bed than to use the hotel safe. Only they must have checked out and forgotten all about it.

Kate unrolled the top of the plastic sack and looked inside, half expecting to find a diamond necklace or perhaps even a wad of cash. But the item she saw shocked her even more.

It was the skirt.

Pulling it out, she blinked at the familiar black fabric in disbelief. It was supposed to be at the bottom of Puget Sound. Not here, in Brock's room.

She looked up at the bathroom door, suddenly aware that both the song and the shower had stopped.

So had her heart.

BROCK EMERGED from the bathroom in a cloud of steam, a towel slung low on his hips. He smiled at Kate, who stood naked beside the bed. He wanted her all over again. Then his gaze dropped to her hand and he saw the skirt clutched in it. One look at her face told him it was over.

"Surprise," she said, her brown eyes bleak.

He swallowed hard. "I think you'd better sit down."

"No, I prefer to stand." She held up the skirt. "Do you want to tell me what this is doing here?"

"Kate." He moved over to her and placed his hand on her elbow, propelling her toward the bed. "Please sit down."

She jerked away from him. "Brock, I'm getting a really bad feeling about this. Tell me now. Tell me it's something perfectly innocent. Tell me you went scuba diving in the Sound and found the skirt. That you wanted to surprise me."

He frantically tried to think of a plausible explanation, but his mind had locked up. All he could think about was losing Kate.

"That's why you taped it under the bed," she continued, the panic rising in her voice. "Because you didn't want me to see it and spoil the surprise. Even though you had no idea I would follow you to your hotel room last night."

He clenched his jaw, realizing he was to blame for the raw pain etched on her beautiful face. But he couldn't lie to her. Not after what had happened between them.

"Tell me," she pleaded, her voice unsteady now. "Tell me before this ruins everything between us."

He raked one hand through his wet hair, swearing harshly under his breath. "I didn't intend for this to happen, Kate. Any of it."

"That doesn't exactly make me feel any better,"

she exclaimed. "I thought last night was special. I thought *we* were special."

"We were," he replied, aware that this was coming out all wrong. "We *are*. Please, Kate, you have to listen to me."

"I will listen. As soon as you say something I can believe. As soon as you explain why you have my skirt." She flung it at him. It hit him in the chest and dropped to the floor. "The skirt I've been searching for ever since it disappeared in that taxi cab. The skirt that I believed was gone forever."

"I know," he said, wanting more than anything to hold her in his arms.

"Were you planning to sell it to Todd?" she asked. "Is that how you knew his company was looking for it?"

"Hell, no," he bit out, then dropped down onto the bed, burying his head in his hands. At last he looked up at her, the sun streaming through the window and casting a golden glow over her gorgeous, naked body. How could he have let this happen? How could he just let it all slip away?

She stood staring at him, waiting for an explanation.

"I could lie to you," he began. "But I won't do that anymore. Not after last night."

"Anymore?" she cried. "You mean you have been lying to me? About what? And for how long?"

He took a deep breath. "About everything. Well, almost everything. Since the first day I came to Seattle."

"That's the day you showed up at my parents' house." Understanding dawned in her eyes. "You didn't expect to find me there, did you, Brock? You didn't expect to find anyone there."

He shook his head, finding this even harder than he had imagined. "I came to Seattle for the skirt. I knew you had it and I wanted to do the job because other people in my field of work, well," he paused, "they usually don't care who gets hurt in the process."

"In case you haven't noticed, Brock," she said, so softly he could barely hear the words. "I'm hurt."

"I mean physically hurt," he clarified, realizing too late that the blow he'd dealt Kate went even deeper.

"Go on."

"My plan was to get in, get the skirt and get out again. You'd never even know I'd been here."

Kate stared at him, looking as if she'd never seen him before. "So you broke into my parents' house to steal the skirt?"

"I didn't think I had any choice."

"Choice?" she cried, throwing her hands in the air. "I'll give you some choices. You could have turned down the job. You could have called me and told me that you'd been hired to steal the skirt. That my parents and I might be in danger from other thieves."

He flinched at the word. "I know I can't make you understand why I lied about my reason for coming here. Or why I paid Carla Corona to lie for me when we tracked the skirt to her house." He saw her wince.

"And you accused Todd of romancing the skirt." She swept her hand over the rumpled bed. "What do you call this? I call it going above and beyond the call of duty!" She drew up her chin. "I hope you're well compensated."

"Damn it, Kate," he said, moving toward her.

But she held up one hand to ward him off. "Don't touch me."

"You don't understand."

"Oh, I understand," she said bleakly. "It was all a game to you."

"No. It was never a game. Especially last night."

She shook her head. "I don't know what to believe anymore."

"Believe me." He wanted to try and find some way to make her understand. "I really thought I was doing it for your own protection. To protect all of you."

She shook her head, sinking down on the bed beside him. "I don't know you," she breathed, pulling the sheet up to cover her nakedness. "I don't know you at all."

"I'm the same man I always was," he replied, realizing that probably wasn't reassuring to her. It was also a lie. "No, that's not true. I'm not the same anymore. I began to change the moment I first saw you standing in your old bedroom. I grew to care more about you than about the mission. About Sid and Rose. That's never happened to me before."

She tightly clasped the sheet to her neck, but didn't say anything.

"I intended to help you find the skirt, Kate." Brock continued. "To let you wear it to the party for your Mr. Right before I took it back to Boston with me. Until I discovered that Mr. Right was Winslow, Mr. All Wrong. For you, anyway."

"Even if that's true," she said, bitterness mingling with her anger, "what gave you the right to decide? To play with all of our lives this way?"

He didn't have an answer for her. Brock hadn't worried about anybody but himself for too long. He'd wanted to protect Kate, but he'd ended up hurting her just the same. His heart contracted at faint shadows under her eyes. They'd barely slept last night, sating themselves on each other and marveling at the almost spiritual connection between them. A connection that had such promise to turn into something more. Something permanent.

"Forget about the past," he implored, reaching for her hand. "It's over. Last night was a new beginning. For both of us."

She turned to look at him, tears gleaming in her eyes. "Last night was a fairy tale. I thought you were my prince." She pulled her hand away from him. "I didn't realize you were just playing the part."

Brock wanted to deny it, but the words stuck in his throat. He watched in silence as she rose to her feet, tugging the sheet off the bed and wrapping it around her. Then she searched the floor of his room for her panties and bra. After she found them, she gathered up the rest of her clothes, including the skirt, and disappeared into the bathroom. A few moments later, she emerged again, fully dressed now, her brown eyes dry, but red-rimmed.

"Don't leave." He couldn't think of what else to say. What else to do.

"I have to," she said, moving to the door, one hand holding the skirt, the other fumbling for the knob. She stood with her back to him. "And I hope you'll do the same. Please leave Seattle as soon as possible. I never want to see you again."

Then she was gone.

16

BROCK SAT unmoving on the bed, waiting for Kate to come back to him. Room service arrived with breakfast, but he let both plates of eggs grow cold, his stomach too knotted with guilt and remorse to eat a single bite. Sunlight streamed through the open drapes and he remembered the way the moonbeams had caressed her body last night. The way she'd given herself to him, body and soul.

By midmorning, he realized she wasn't coming back—ever. He'd blown it. Really blown it. And for what? A mission. A job he didn't even care about anymore.

But it was all he had left.

He picked up the telephone and dialed the number for Dooley's, his entire body feeling numb. One of the waitresses answered. "Is Dooley in yet?"

He heard the waitress yell for her boss. It seemed like a lifetime ago since he'd been there, when in reality it had only been a couple of weeks. But his life had changed in that time. He'd changed.

Dooley got on the line. "Hey, Brock. I didn't expect to hear from you again so soon. What's up?"

"Is that job in Rio still available?"

Dooley hesitated. "Why? Are you interested?"

"I can leave today." He waited for Dooley to ask him about the status of the skirt. But to his surprise, the subject didn't even come up.

"Well, I've already sent Bryant down there to assess the situation. But to tell you the truth, it's more of a two-man job. I'll have a ticket waiting for you at the Seatac airport."

Brock's throat was so tight, he didn't trust himself to speak. He swallowed hard. A long moment of silence stretched between them.

"You okay?" Dooley asked at last.

"I will be," Brock replied, though he didn't believe it. He'd never be okay again. He hung up the phone and got dressed. Then he packed his few belongings and made preparations to check out of the hotel. He'd leave Seattle behind. Leave Kate behind. And try like hell to put her out of his mind. But he knew in his gut that was one mission he'd never be able to accomplish.

Brock looked around the room, certain he'd forgotten something. He spotted a memo pad on top of the television set, then searched the room until he found a pencil. He tried not to think about how much fun it had been waking up with her this morning. He'd never realized how lonely he'd been until Kate had come back into his life.

He jotted down one simple word, then tore the top sheet off the memo pad and stuffed it into his shirt pocket. Picking up his suitcase, he headed for the door.

There was only one thing left to do.

KATE WALKED through most of the day in a daze. She opened her office early, desperate to get her mind off Brock. But neither her mind nor her heart were in her work. While she organized a brunch meeting for a group of architects, her mind kept flashing back to moments with Brock. Standing with him in the telephone booth. The way he'd picked her up in his arms last night. The expression on his face this morning when he saw her holding the skirt.

She spent the morning fighting back tears and the afternoon fueling her anger. She'd need that anger to sustain her if he didn't take her advice and leave Seattle. As of noon, he still hadn't checked out of the hotel.

Kate cleaned off her desk, more out of nervous energy than necessity. She glanced at the clock on the wall, surprised to find it was already after four o'clock. Only three more hours until the party. Sid and Rose had both agreed to meet her for dinner at the Harbor Room at the hotel, neither aware that the other was coming. Or that there would be a huge party in their honor.

Maybe it was a mistake to throw them together in this situation. She'd learned much too recently that love was more complicated than she'd ever imagined.

Then another thought occurred to her. What if Brock showed up? It would take some nerve, especially if he was still trying to make excuses. Yet, part of her ached at the thought of never seeing him again.

Kate opened another file drawer and drew out an emergency box of Twinkies, hoping to find solace in empty calories. She tore open the cellophane wrapper, then turned around and saw a man standing in the office doorway.

"Tony," she gasped, her mouth full of cake and cream.

He grinned. "Eating again, I see."

She set down the Twinkies and rounded the desk, flying into her big brother's arms for a hug. He looked healthy and tanned and more like Sid Talavera than ever. "When did you get here?"

"Elena and I flew in this afternoon. We checked into our room about an hour ago and she's taking a much needed nap. So I decided this was the perfect time to check up on my little sister."

She squeezed him tight, the big brother she hadn't

seen for over three years. The one person who knew Brock better than anyone—even her. "I'm so glad you're here."

"Hey, you okay?" he said, squeezing her back.

"I've just really missed you." A lump rose in her throat and she swallowed hard to contain it. She wasn't about to pour out all her troubles thirty seconds after he arrived.

Stepping back, she gave him a watery smile. "So how's Elena? And congratulations on the baby! I'm so excited to be an aunt. I know Mom and Dad will be so thrilled when they hear the news."

"Elena is doing great. No morning sickness or anything. It's amazing, Kate," his voice softened with awe. "The fact that she and I created a child together. My wife is more beautiful now than ever."

That did it. The tears overflowed and poured down her cheeks. She drew in a deep breath, sobs hiccuping in her throat. "That's wonderful."

Tony's brows drew together in a puzzled frown. "What is it, Katie? You never cry. Is there something wrong? Something I should know about?"

She took another deep breath, trying to regain control. "Well, Mom and Dad are separated. I didn't tell you because I thought, and hoped, they'd be back together by now."

Tony slumped against the wall. "Separated? How could that happen?"

"It's a long story. Brock and I did our best to try and bring them back together, but you know how stubborn they both can be. And they still don't know about the anniversary party, although they'll find out when they show up here tonight." She paused to catch her breath. "Do you think that's a mistake?"

"I think it's got disaster written all over it." Then he straightened. "Wait a minute. Did you say Brock? As in Brock Gannon?"

She nodded, pressing her lips together to keep them from trembling. This was ridiculous. She wasn't the weepy type. And she hardly ever lost control.

"What's he doing here?"

"He came for the party and..."

"And?" Tony prodded.

She squared her shoulders. "And I've asked him to leave, but he hasn't checked out yet, so I'd like you to go up to his room and kick him out."

Tony folded his arms across his chest. "All right, Kate. Spill it. What the hell is really going on here?"

The memory of Brock's betrayal dried the tears in her eyes and sparked her anger once more. "Your friend lied to me, among other things. It's another long story and it doesn't have a happy ending."

Tony stared at her, his eyes widening with sudden comprehension. "You're in love with the guy."

"I've never had the best taste in men. I'm sure I'll

get over it." But Kate wasn't sure at all. Even after all
Brock had done to her, she still yearned to hold him
in her arms. To feel the passion of his kisses and the
warmth of his body against her own.

"So what exactly did he do to you?"

Kate blushed, until she realized Tony wasn't talking about last night. "You mean, besides lying to me
and coming to Seattle under false pretenses? Well,
for starters, he tried to dictate who I could date."

Tony smiled. "Can't exactly blame him for that. As
you just said, you haven't always had the best taste
in men."

"Except that I finally met Mr. Perfect, at least I
think he's Mr. Perfect. Well, you know him—Todd
Winslow, our old neighbor." Kate threw her hands
up in the air, breaking her vow not to get worked up
again. "For absolutely no reason whatsoever, Brock
decides that Todd is all wrong for me. Practically for-
bids me to date him!"

"I know the reason," Tony said calmly.

She blinked at him. "You do?"

"Sure," Tony replied, then he hesitated. "Gannon
never wanted you to know, and I agreed with him at
the time. But maybe now it would be better for you to
find out the truth. Then at least you'd understand
Brock's motives."

"What truth? Is this about the fight between Brock
and Todd in high school?"

"I wouldn't exactly call it a fight," Tony replied. "Winslow never even got a chance to throw a punch. Brock beat the tar out of him. The guy's lucky he only suffered three cracked ribs, two black eyes, and one severely bruised ego. I've never seen Gannon so worked up."

"About what?" Kate asked, wishing her brother would get on with it already.

"About you." Tony scowled. "Mr. Perfect Next-Door Neighbor was a damn Peeping Tom. He took pictures of you sunbathing in our backyard and showed them off to all the guys in the locker rooms. Hate to tell you, sis, but they weren't flattering pictures."

Her cheeks burned, remembering all the times she'd stuffed herself into a tiny bikini as a teenager in an effort to get a beautiful golden tan. As if that would conceal the extra fifty pounds she'd carried around. Todd would have had to climb that old oak tree in his backyard to get a view of her over the privacy fence surrounding the Talavera property.

"Winslow was really on a roll by the time Brock and I walked into the locker room," Tony said. "He was calling you Katie the Whale and making really crude comments about uses for blubber."

She closed her eyes, mortified for the insecure, overweight teenager she'd been. It would have killed her to learn the truth. Or at least, made her drop out of school.

"Brock was on top of Winslow before I could even react. In fact, I was the one who had to pull him off the guy before he killed him." Tony's mouth thinned. "Not that I wasn't tempted to finish the job myself."

Katie couldn't believe she'd been so clueless. "How could I not know this? Did Mom and Dad know?"

Tony shook his head. "When the school called in the Winslows, they wanted to bring in the police. Until they learned the reason Brock had attacked their son. Let's just say they weren't thrilled with Todd's behavior. And they didn't want to cause trouble in the neighborhood, so they ultimately decided not to press charges."

"But Brock still got kicked out of school," Kate said softly. "Because of me."

"Yeah. And I've never heard him say he regretted it. Not once."

It shouldn't change anything, but she knew that it did. Her anger shifted to something less volatile. Something full of possibilities—and understanding. At least now she knew why Brock had been so adamant about her staying away from Todd Winslow.

She let the news about Todd's old behavior sink in, trying to gauge her reaction. To her surprise, she found it was relief. A tangible reason for her to walk away from Todd. Not because of what had happened all those years ago—teenagers did all sorts of stupid things. But because she knew what love really was now. And she couldn't settle for anything less.

She and Tony talked for awhile longer, catching up on each other's lives and worrying about the state of their parents' marriage. When he finally left to check on Elena, Kate locked up her office and raced to her room. The first thing she did was pick up the telephone and dial Brock's room. She wasn't sure she was ready to forgive him—his betrayal still hurt. But at least now she was ready to finally listen to him. Really listen, with her heart as well as her head.

She let the telephone ring fifteen times before she finally gave up. The anniversary party was due to start soon and she needed to get there early to make certain everything was running smoothly. She'd have to worry about repairing her relationship with Brock later.

Moving to her closet, she pulled out the outfit she was planning to wear, then froze when she saw an empty white plastic clothes hanger on the rod. The one she'd hung the skirt on this morning. Only the skirt was missing. A note was threaded through the plastic hook. It had one simple word on it, written with a man's bold hand. *Sorry.*

She ran to the phone and hastily dialed the front

desk. "Mr. Gannon checked out an hour ago," the desk clerk informed her.

Kate hung up the phone, disappointment and disbelief welling up inside of her. The skirt was gone.

And so was Brock.

17

THE PARTY was in full swing by 7:30 p.m. that evening, but the guests of honor still hadn't arrived. Kate stationed Tony by the door as a lookout, then placed a telephone call to her father's house. There was no answer, which made her hope he was on his way.

"Are you sure Mom is coming?" Kate asked her Aunt Flora, who was already on her third glass of champagne.

"Positive," Flora replied. "And you don't know how hard it was to keep this party a secret from her. Although, I'm still not sure that was a good idea. I don't know how she'll react when she sees Sid. She was quite upset last night."

Kate didn't know either. Maybe she'd been too cavalier about her parents' problems. Now she knew how complicated it was to love someone. How fragile a relationship could be. But it was too late now. The guests were all gathered here and ready to celebrate Sid and Rose Talavera's forty years of wedded bliss.

Knowing she had to muddle through the evening, Kate started across the large hall to greet her grandparents. But Todd Winslow stepped in her way.

"Hello, Kate," he said, his gaze moving appreciatively over her. "You look wonderful. I've been wanting to talk to you all day."

"Hi, Todd." She didn't tell him she'd been avoiding his phone calls. Ever since she'd learned about his Peeping Tom stunt, he'd lost his golden glow.

He took a step closer to her, eminently dashing in his olive-green suit. "I'm happy to see Gannon's not here. It should be a much better party without him."

An empty ache filled her chest. "I'm sorry last night ended so abruptly Todd. I never had a chance to thank you for a lovely evening."

He smiled, then leaned toward her ear. "You can thank me by having a drink with me after the party. I realized last night how much I've come to care for you, Kate. I want to talk about our future."

This was it. The moment she'd dreamed about for so long. "I'm sorry, Todd," she said, feeling no remorse. "That won't be possible."

His brow creased. "Because of what Gannon told you? Don't let him come between us, Kate. I think we could really have something special."

"Maybe we could have," she said gently. "Once. But I'm in love with another man. I'm sorry, Todd. I hope someday you find the woman you're looking for."

He stared at her for a long moment. "I'm sorry, too." Then he turned and walked away.

She watched him, realizing she'd seen genuine disappointment in his eyes. He'd changed in the past twelve years. So had she. So why had it been so impossible for her to believe Brock had changed, too? He'd come to Seattle to search for the skirt, but he'd done so much more. Spending time with her father and helping her plan the party.

Warning her about Todd.

None of those things had helped him accomplish his mission. Yet, he'd been there for her when she'd needed him. And he'd made love to her as if he really meant it. No man had ever held her that way before or made her feel so cherished. How could she just let him walk away? No, she reminded herself, she'd done worse than that. She'd told him to leave.

And he'd taken the skirt with him.

Kate heard her name drift over the crowd and turned toward the entrance. Her brother Tony was waving to her, signaling that their parents had arrived. She hurried to the door, wanting to prepare them before they stepped into the room. But Sid was the only one standing in the foyer, wearing his new suit.

"Dad," she said, after a warning glance from Tony,

who stood behind the wide door frame, still hidden from his father's view. "When did you get here?"

"Just now." He craned his neck to look around her. "Is that my cousin Joe in there?"

She took a step towards him. "Yes, it is. Now, Dad, don't get upset."

"Upset?" Sid echoed. "Why would I get upset? What's going on here, Katie?"

"This is a surprise fortieth anniversary party for you and Mom."

He gaped at her. "Oh, no."

"Oh, yes," she replied. "It's been planned for months. Maybe I should have canceled it when you and Mom separated, but I really believed you'd be reconciled by now."

Sid heaved a sigh. "I'm not sure that will ever happen."

"Don't say that," she said, moving toward him. "Maybe a night like this is just what you two need. With people here who love you. Who all know how much you two belong together."

"But your mother's not even here," he said, a flush mottling his cheeks. "Is she?"

Kate hesitated. "Not yet."

"I'll look like a fool if I walk into that party alone."

"I'm sure she'll be here soon."

Sid didn't look as confident. "How long do you expect me to wait?"

"At least a few minutes more, Dad. Please."

Ten long minutes passed and there was still no sign of Rose. Sid paced back and forth across the pink floral carpet in the foyer. Music reverberated from the party room and the tantalizing aromas of the hors d'oeurves filled the air.

"That's it," Sid exclaimed at last, his face drawn. "I think Rose has made it perfectly clear how she feels about our marriage." He turned to leave.

"Dad, wait," Kate implored, grabbing his arm. "Mom didn't even know you were going to be here. This party will be as much of a surprise to her as it was to you."

"Not if she doesn't show up."

"Aunt Flora promised me she'd be here."

"Maybe your mother saw me and turned around and left. How much longer do you expect me to stand out here?"

Her brother rounded the doorway. "As long as it takes, Dad."

"Tony!" Sid advanced on his son, enveloping him in a big bear hug. "What are you doing here?"

"I came to help celebrate your wedding anniversary. Elena's here, too. She's right inside."

Sid clapped his hand on his son's shoulder. "It's so good to see you again, son. It's been much too long."

"Sounds like I came back in the nick of time," Tony replied. "What's the deal with you and Mom? I couldn't believe it when Katie told me you two were separated."

"It wasn't my choice," Sid informed him, a stubborn set to his jaw. "Your mother is the one who left. It's up to her to come back."

Kate turned to her brother. "Mom is just as stubborn as he is. Neither one of them will budge an inch."

"I'm too old to change now," Sid said. "Too set in my ways. I guess I'm just not the man your mother wants now." He sighed. "I don't know what happened. I just know we're not twenty years old anymore."

"Sid?"

All three of them turned to see Rose standing in the foyer. She wore a white blouse with a full lace collar and a black skirt. A very familiar black skirt. Kate's mouth dropped open when she realized who must have given it to her.

Sid gaped at his wife, then slowly walked toward her, mesmerized. At last he spoke. "Rose, you look..." His voice trailed off as he stared at her, speechless.

She slowly turned for him, giving her husband the full view. "I wore this especially for you, Sid." She touched her fingers to the lacy collar of her blouse. "Do you recognize it?"

He nodded, his gaze never leaving her face. "You wore it on our first date."

She smiled. "I was a little overdressed for a baseball game."

"You were beautiful," Sid countered. "Almost as beautiful as you are now."

Rose blushed. "I suddenly have an incredible craving for hot dogs."

Sid reached for her hand and pulled her into his arms. "You'll have to wait. I think they're playing our song."

Kate watched her parents dance together as the romantic strains of "I Can't Stop Loving You" drifted into the foyer. They moved slowly to the music, their cheeks pressed together, their eyes closed.

Tony and Kate exchanged glances, then both silently left the foyer and re-entered the party room.

"Congratulations, sis," he said, circling his arm around her shoulders and giving her a squeeze. "Looks like we may have something to celebrate after all."

Kate nodded, then looked at the band, wondering how they'd had such perfect timing. She saw the reason standing across the room. *Brock.* He leaned against the bandstand, his black suitcoat open to reveal a crisp white shirt and a red silk tie. One hand was tucked into the front pocket of his black slacks.

He hadn't left after all.

Her throat tightened as he caught her gaze. He held it for a long moment, then straightened and slowly started toward her across the dance floor.

She met him halfway, her heart racing in her chest.

"Let me explain before you throw me out," he began, his voice low and fervent.

"I think it's all pretty clear," she replied.

He shook his head. "It wasn't to me. Not until I'd made plans to fly to Rio. To fly away from the woman I love. Then I realized this mission wasn't over."

"You still needed the skirt."

He nodded. "I knew you didn't need that skirt to win Todd Winslow. The guy is wild about you. Why else do you think seeing the two of you together makes me so crazy?"

"So you took the skirt from my room."

"Sid and Rose needed something to break down that wall of stubbornness between them. I thought that skirt might be just the thing to do it."

"It worked," she said, aware that couples were dancing all around them while they stood still in the center of the dance floor. It was as if her whole life had come to a standstill. "Mission accomplished."

He moved a step closer to her. "Not quite. I still don't have you."

She didn't say anything, not trusting herself to speak. Her connection to him felt so fragile at this moment. So precarious. What if she said the wrong thing? What if he did?

"We talked about choices before," he said, gazing intently into her eyes. "I've made too many wrong choices. Except one—falling in love with you. Although, that wasn't really a choice. I think it was my destiny."

She licked her dry lips. "And what about my choices?"

His gaze flicked to Todd, who stood by the champagne fountain, chatting with his parents. When Brock looked back at her, his eyes were stormy, but resigned. "If nothing else, I hope you'll choose to be my friend."

"I'm sorry." She took a deep breath. "That's not possible."

His face fell. "Kate," he began, but she held up one hand to forestall him.

"I have to be more than your friend, Brock," she explained, taking a step closer to him, until their bodies were almost touching. She looked up into his eyes. "Because I want you when I wake up in the morning. I want you when I go to bed every night. And the wanting just gets worse in between. But there's one more reason I could never be just your friend."

"Kate," he breathed, reaching for her.

"I love you, Brock," she said, right before he kissed her.

She wound her arms around his neck, sinking into him. He held her so tightly she could barely breathe.

At last he lifted his head. "You have another choice to make." He took a deep breath. "Marry me, Kate."

She smiled, joy bubbling up inside of her. "That's the easiest one yet. Yes, Brock, I'll marry you."

He whooped with delight, swooping her up off the floor and twirling her around in his arms. Then he set her down, a goofy grin on his face. "Okay, one more choice. When? The sooner, the better, in my opinion."

"This time, I'll let you choose," she said, catching a glimpse of her mother and father dancing by them. They were oblivious to the fact that their daughter had just become engaged. They only had eyes for each other.

"Okay," Brock replied. "I choose April tenth. The day we first met fourteen years ago."

She gaped up at him in disbelief. "You remember the exact day?"

"April 10, 1988," he said, reaching out to tweak one long curl. "You wore pigtails. I thought you were cute."

She laughed. "You wore a black leather jacket. I thought you were dangerous."

His voice grew husky. "I didn't know the meaning of the word danger until I saw you all grown up."

"It was the skirt," she told him.

"It was you," he countered.

She walked into his arms, knowing it was exactly where she belonged. "It was fate."

_____Epilogue_____

THE CROWD of women thronged into the ballroom at the hotel, at least five times as many as had been invited to the wedding reception.

Gwen, Torrie and Chelsea stood with Kate between them, wearing bridesmaids dresses designed by Daryl, the hottest new designer on the east coast. Each held the single pink rose they'd carried in the wedding ceremony.

"Can you believe this madhouse?" Chelsea said, shaking her head in disbelief.

"I take it the word is out in Seattle about the skirt." Gwen smiled. "Bachelors beware."

"Thanks to my Aunt Flora." Kate reached up to adjust her short veil. She wore her mother's wedding gown, a Grace Kelly style bubble sheath with long sleeves and a banded waist. She had the skirt folded over her arm, ready for the next recipient.

"What did she do?" Torrie asked. "Put out a news bulletin about the skirt?"

"Worse," Kate replied. "Aunt Flora told her

bridge club about the skirt's part in my parents' reconciliation."

Chelsea fingered the skirt. "I wonder who will wear it next?"

Kate did too. She'd offered to give it to Brock so he could complete his mission, but Dooley told them the client had backed out of the deal after losing a close election.

But Kate had other things on her mind. Like starting her honeymoon. Brock was taking her to Boston to meet Dooley, then on to Martha's Vineyard. She searched the crowd for her new husband, finally spotting him in deep conversation with her father.

Sid had given Rose a special anniversary present, a six month cruise around the world. Her father was actually looking forward to the trip, now that Brock had agreed to take over the business. Talavera Construction was now Talavera and Gannon Construction.

Another perfect union.

Then Brock looked at her and Kate forgot everything except how much she loved him. She smiled and nodded at him, watching him walk over to confer with the bandleader.

"Attention, everyone," the bandleader announced over the microphone. "It's now time for the bride to toss the bouquet.... No, wait a minute. What?"

Kate saw Brock set the guy straight.

"Oh, my mistake," the bandleader announced. "The bride will be tossing a skirt. I repeat, a skirt." He looked at his fellow musicians and rolled his eyes. "So now is the time for all you lovely single women to gather in the center of the ballroom floor. Don't be shy."

The crowd of eager women surged forward. Kate and her three bridesmaids stepped up onto the circular dais to avoid the mob.

"Can you believe it?" Chelsea murmured. "Only four months ago, that was us out there. Who knew I'd have Zach McDaniels in my future."

"Or Alec Fleming in mine," Gwen said.

"I never imagined Brock Gannon coming back into my life." Kate grinned as her husband looked purposefully at his watch, then winked at her. "But I'm so glad he did."

The women hugged each other, the skirt caught between them.

Then the crowd began to chant. "Skirt! Skirt! Skirt!"

The three friends drew apart and Kate stepped forward. Some of the faces looking up at her were hopeful. Some expectant. A few desperate. She took a deep breath, knowing she held someone's future in her hands. But now it was time to start her own.

Then she tossed the skirt high into the air....

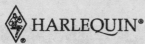

This Mother's Day
Give Your Mom
A Royal Treat

Win a fabulous one-week vacation in
Puerto Rico for you and your mother at
the luxurious Inter-Continental San Juan
Resort & Casino. The prize includes round
trip airfare for two, breakfast daily and a
mother and daughter day of beauty
at the beachfront hotel's spa.

INTER·CONTINENTAL
San Juan
RESORT & CASINO

Here's all you have to do:

Tell us in 100 words or less how your
mother helped with the romance in your
life. It may be a story about your engagement,
wedding or those boyfriends when you were
a teenager or any other romantic advice
from your mother. The entry will be judged
based on its originality, emotionally
compelling nature and sincerity.
See official rules on following page.

Send your entry to:
Mother's Day Contest

In Canada
P.O. Box 637
Fort Erie, Ontario
L2A 5X3

In U.S.A.
P.O. Box 9076
3010 Walden Ave.
Buffalo, NY
14269-9076

Or enter online at www.eHarlequin.com

All entries must be postmarked by April 1, 2002.
Winner will be announced May 1, 2002. Contest open to
Canadian and U.S. residents who are 18 years of age and older.
No purchase necessary to enter. Void where prohibited.

PRROY

Two ways to enter:

• **Via The Internet:** Log on to the Harlequin romance website (www.eHarlequin.com) anytime beginning 12:01 a.m. E.S.T., January 1, 200° through 11:59 p.m. E.S.T., April 1, 2002 and follow the directions displayed on-line to enter your name, address (including zip code), e-mail address and in 100 words or fewer, describe how your mother helped with the romance in your life.

• **Via Mail:** Handprint (or type) on an 8 1/2" x 11" plain piece of paper, your name, address (including zip code) and e-mail address (if you h one), and in 100 words or fewer, describe how your mother helped with the romance in your life. Mail your entry via first-class mail to: Harleq Mother's Day Contest 2216, (in the U.S.) P.O. Box 9076, Buffalo, NY 14269-9076; (in Canada) P.O. Box 637, Fort Erie, Ontario, Canada L2A

For eligibility, entries must be submitted either through a completed Internet transmission or postmarked no later than 11:59 p.m. E.S.T., April 1, 2 (mail-in entries must be received by April 9, 2002). Limit one entry per person, household address and e-mail address. On-line and/or mailed entries received from persons residing in geographic areas in which entry is not permissible will be disqualified.

Entries will be judged by a panel of judges, consisting of members of the Harlequin editorial, marketing and public relations staff using the following crit
  • Originality - 50%
  • Emotional Appeal - 25%
  • Sincerity - 25%

In the event of a tie, duplicate prizes will be awarded. Decisions of the judges are final.

Prize: A 6-night/7-day stay for two at the Inter-Continental San Juan Resort & Casino, including round-trip coach air transportation from gatewa airport nearest winner's home (approximate retail value: $4,000). Prize includes breakfast daily and a mother and daughter day of beauty at t beachfront hotel's spa. Prize consists of only those items listed as part of the prize. Prize is valued in U.S. currency.

All entries become the property of Torstar Corp. and will not be returned. No responsibility is assumed for lost, late, illegible, incomplete, inaccura non-delivered or misdirected mail or misdirected e-mail, for technical, hardware or software failures of any kind, lost or unavailable network connections, or failed, incomplete, garbled or delayed computer transmission or any human error which may occur in the receipt or processing e entries in this Contest.

Contest open only to residents of the U.S. (except Colorado) and Canada, who are 18 years of age or older and is void wherever prohibited by all applicable laws and regulations apply. Any litigation within the Province of Quebec respecting the conduct or organization of a publicity conte may be submitted to the Régie des alcools, des courses et des jeux for a ruling. Any litigation respecting the awarding of a prize may be submi to the Régie des alcools, des courses et des jeux only for the purpose of helping the parties reach a settlement. Employees and immediate fami members of Torstar Corp. and D.L. Blair, Inc., their affiliates, subsidiaries and all other agencies, entities and persons connected with the use, marketing or conduct of this Contest are not eligible to enter. Taxes on prize are the sole responsibility of winner. Acceptance of any prize offer constitutes permission to use winner's name, photograph or other likeness for the purposes of advertising, trade and promotion on behalf of To Corp., its affiliates and subsidiaries without further compensation to the winner, unless prohibited by law.

Winner will be determined no later than April 15, 2002 and be notified by mail. Winner will be required to sign and return an Affidavit of Eligib form within 15 days after winner notification. Non-compliance within that time period may result in disqualification and an alternate winner ma selected. Winner of trip must execute a Release of Liability prior to ticketing and must possess required travel documents (e.g. Passport, photo where applicable. Travel must be completed within 12 months of selection and is subject to traveling companion completing and returning a Re of Liability prior to travel; and hotel and flight accommodations availability. Certain restrictions and blackout dates may apply. No substitution o permitted by winner. Torstar Corp. and D.L. Blair, Inc., their parents, affiliates, and subsidiaries are not responsible for errors in printing or electr presentation of Contest, or entries. In the event of printing or other errors which may result in unintended prize values or duplication of prizes, affected entries shall be null and void. If for any reason the Internet portion of the Contest is not capable of running as planned, including infec by computer virus, bugs, tampering, unauthorized intervention, fraud, technical failures, or any other causes beyond the control of Torstar Corp. which corrupt or affect the administration, secrecy, fairness, integrity or proper conduct of the Contest, Torstar Corp. reserves the right, at its sol discretion, to disqualify any individual who tampers with the entry process and to cancel, terminate, modify or suspend the Contest or the Inter portion thereof. In the event the Internet portion must be terminated a notice will be posted on the website and all entries received prior to termination will be judged in accordance with these rules. In the event of a dispute regarding an on-line entry, the entry will be deemed submitt by the authorized holder of the e-mail account submitted at the time of entry. Authorized account holder is defined as the natural person who i assigned to an e-mail address by an Internet access provider, on-line service provider or other organization that is responsible for arranging e-ma address for the domain associated with the submitted e-mail address. Torstar Corp. and/or D.L. Blair Inc. assumes no responsibility for any com injury or damage related to or resulting from accessing and/or downloading any sweepstakes material. Rules are subject to any requirements/ limitations imposed by the FCC. **Purchase or acceptance of a product offer does not improve your chances of winning.**

For winner's name (available after May 1, 2002), send a self-addressed, stamped envelope to: Harlequin Mother's Day Contest Winners 2216 P.O. Box 4200 Blair, NE 68009-4200 or you may access the www.eHarlequin.com Web site through June 3, 2002.

Contest sponsored by Torstar Corp., P.O. Box 9042, Buffalo, NY 14269-9042.